The Moving Finger

Mary Gaunt

Alpha Editions

This edition published in 2023

ISBN : 9789357957038

Design and Setting By
Alpha Editions
www.alphaedis.com
Email - info@alphaedis.com

Contents

TROTTING COB

"Hi—hey—hold up there, mare, will you? What did you say, mister? A light? Yes. That 's Trotting Cob, that is. The missus 'll give us a cup of tea, but that's about all. Devil fly away with the mare. What is it? Something white in the road? Water by ———. Thank the Lord, they 've had plenty of rain this year. But they do say there's a ghost hereabouts—a Trotting Cob, with a man in white on him? Lord, no, that's an old woman's tale. But the girl—she walks—she walks they say, and mighty good reason—too—if all tales be true. Hosses always shy here if they 've at all skittish. Got that letter, Jack, and the tobacco? That's right! Rum, isn't it, to get all your news of the world at dead of night? Reg'ler as clockwork we pass—a little after one, and the coach from Deniliquin she passes an hour or so earlier.

"Anybody else? Well, no, not as a rule. It's the stock route? you see, between Hay and Deniliquin, so there's bound to be stock on the way; but sheep, bless you! they travel six miles a day, and cattle they ain't so much faster, so we brings 'em all the news. The Company has stables here, and feed, and we change horses. The old man and old woman keep it, with a boy or two. Mighty dull for the old woman, I should think, with on'y the ghost to keep her company. She was her cousin or her aunt or somethin', the ghost was, and, Lord, women is fools an' no mistake." It was July, and the winter rains had just fallen, so that the plains, contrary to custom, were a regular sea of mud.

The wheels sank axle deep in it. The horses floundered through it in the darkness, and every now and then the lamps were reflected in a big pool of shallow water. The wind blew keen and cold, but the coach was full inside and out, and so, though it was pitch dark, I kept my seat by the driver.

A light gleamed up out of the darkness.

"Trotting Cob!" said he, and discoursed upon it till he pulled up his horses on their haunches exactly opposite a wide-open door, where the lamplight displayed a rudely-laid table and a bright fire, which seemed hospitably to beckon us in. The whole place was as wide awake as if it were noon instead of midnight.

Ten minutes' stay, and we were off again into the darkness, and then I prevailed upon the driver to tell me the tale of Trotting Cob. He told it in his own way. He interlarded his speech with strange oaths. He stopped often to swear at the road, to correct the horses, and he was emphatic in his opinions on the foolishness of women, so I must e'en do as he did, and tell the tale of Trotting Cob in my own way.

A flat world—possibly to English eyes an uninteresting, desolate, dreary world; but to those who knew and loved them, they had a weird charm, all their own, those dull, gray plains that stretched away mile after mile till it seemed the horizon, unbroken by hill or tree, must be the end of the world. Trotting Cob was Murwidgee then, Murwidgee Waterhole, where all the stock stopped and watered; but from the slab hut, which was the only dwelling for miles, no waterhole was visible; the creek was simply a huge crack in the earth, and at the bottom, twenty feet below the level of the plain, was the water-hole. One waterhole in summer, and in winter a whole chain of them, but the creek seldom if ever flowed, except in a very wet season. It was a permanent waterhole—Murwidgee, fed by springs, and the white cockatoos and screaming corellas came there and bathed in its waters, and the black swans, and the wild duck, and teal rested there on their way south, when summer had laid his iron hand on the northern plains.

The reeds and rushes made a pleasant green patch in the creek bed, and once there had been several tall white gums; but old Durham had cut them down years ago, when first he settled there, and so from the hut door, though almost close upon the creek, it was not visible, and there was presented to the eye an unbroken expanse of salt bush. It was unbroken but for the mirage that quivered in the dry, hot air. The lake of shining water, with the ferns and trees reflected in it, was but a phantasy, and the girl who leaned idly against the door-post of the hut knew it. Still she looked at it wistfully—it had been so hot, so cruelly hot, this burning January day, and in all the wide plain that stretched away for miles on every side there was not a particle of shade; even the creek ran north and south, so that the hot sun sought out every nook and corner, and the bark-roofed hut, with its few tumble-down outbuildings, was uncompromisingly hot, desolate, and ugly.

Old Durham called himself a squatter, and gave out that his wife, with the help of her granddaughter Nellie, kept an accommodation-house. Forty years ago the times were wild, and what did it matter. Convict and thief the squatters round called him, and his grandsons, in their opinion, were the most accomplished cattle-duffers in all the country round, and as for the accommodation-house—well, if the old woman did go in for sly grog-selling, the police were a long way off, and it was no business of anybody's. And Nellie Durham was a pretty girl, a little simple perhaps, but still sweetly pretty, with those wistful blue eyes, fringed with dark lashes, that looked out at you so earnestly, and the wealth of fair hair. So dainty and so pretty—the coarse cotton gown was quite forgotten, and in those times, when women of any sort were scarce, many a man turned out of his way just to speak a word or two to Mother Durham's granddaughter.

She sat down on the door-step now, and resting her elbows on her knees, and her chin in her hands, looked out across the plain. The sun was just setting—a fiery, glowing sun, that sent long, level beams right across the plains, till they reached her hair, and turned it to living gold, and went on and penetrated the gloom of the hut beyond.

It was very bare, the hut, just as bare as it could possibly be; but three men bent eagerly over the rough-hewn table, while an old woman, worn and wrinkled and haggard, and yet in whose face might still be traced a ghastly resemblance to the pretty girl outside, laid out on the table a much-thumbed, dirty pack of cards.

"Cut them, Bill. Drat you! what 'd you do that for, George? You know you ain't never lucky—you oughter let Bill do it. No—no—no luck. Two, three, nine o' spades, 'tis ill luck all through."

"Well, let Bill do it, Gran," said George with an oath, as he flung down the cards, and they were picked up and shuffled, and cut again and again; the old woman shook her head solemnly.

"'Tis bad luck the night," she said, "bad, bad luck. Don't you touch Macartney's mob, or you 'll rue it. There's death some-wheres, but it doesn't point to none o' you."

"Macartney probably," said another man, who was leaning against the slab wall, and intently watching the girl in the doorway. "Come, Gran, don't be croaking; if the cards ain't lucky, put 'em away till they are."

He looked cleaner and smarter than the other three—Nellie's brothers, who were young fellows, little over twenty. They were good-looking, strapping fellows, but the sweet simplicity in her face was in theirs loutish stupidity, and their companion stood out beside them, though probably he was nearly twice their age, as cast in a very different mould. He was dressed as they were, in riding-breeches and shirt, but the shirt was clean, his black hair and beard were neatly trimmed, the sash round his waist was new and neatly folded, and the pistols therein were bright and well kept. Gentleman Jim, the Durhams called him; as Gentleman Jim he was known to the police throughout all the length and breadth of New South Wales. What he had been once no man knew, though evidently he was a man of some little culture and education; what he was now was patent to every man—escaped convict, bushranger, cattle-duffer—even a murder now and again, it was whispered, came not amiss to Gentleman Jim. It was an evil face, with the handsome dark eyes set too closely together, and when there is evil in a man's face at forty, there is surely little hope for him; but bad as it was, to Nellie Durham it was the one face in the world. Cattle-duffing—it hardly seemed a sin to her. Ever since she could remember, her grandfather, and her father, and when he died, her brothers, had driven off a few head of cattle from the mobs that passed, and she in her simplicity hardly realized the heinousness of the offence; and for the rest, she simply believed nothing against her hero. He had been cruelly ill-treated, cruelly ill-used, but she understood him—she loved him, she believed in him, in the blind unreasoning way a woman, be she old or young, rich or poor, wise or foolish, gentle or simple, does believe in the man she loves. And the old grandmother saw, and shook her head. She did not mind cattle-duffing—it was but levying a fair toll on the rich squatter as he passed. Sly grog-selling was hardly a crime; so few people passed it would have been waste of money to take out a licence, more especially since there was no one to ask whether they had one or not. But Gentleman Jim, whom the boys had taken to bringing home with them of late, was another matter altogether, and she looked on anxiously when she saw the impression he had made on her son's pretty daughter.

"I dunno," she said, anxiously to her husband, "whether the gal's all there; sometimes I think she ain't, but anyhow, she's sweet and pretty an' loving, an' he's an out-an'-out scamp, drat him!"

But the old man would not interfere. He was a little afraid of Gentleman Jim; besides he was useful to him—he was getting old, and the grandsons were not much help; they took after their mother, and privately old Durham thought his son's wife had been more than half a fool, so he encouraged Gentleman Jim; and now came information that Macartney would be camping here to-morrow with a mob ready for the southern market, and here was the man again. The cards too prophesied disaster, shuffle them as she would.

Gentleman Jim swore at the cards and at the old woman in no measured terms, and then he laughed, and gathered them up in his hands.

"Here, Nell, Nell!—the cards are clean against us, your Gran says—come and cut, like a good girl."

Nellie rose willingly enough, but the old woman said scornfully, "Nell, Nell, she ain't got no luck at all. Three times I tried her fortune, and three times it came, 'tears, tears, tears'—never naught else for Nell but tears."

"Never mind, mother, better luck this time, eh, Nell?" and the girl took the cards, and smiled trustingly up into his face.

"Cut, Nell."

She cut the nine of spades, and the old woman groaned. "Disaster, sure as fate; let Macartney's mob alone, I tell you."

"Cut again, Nell."

She shuffled them carefully, the other four watching her with eager, anxious eyes, while the man at her side looked on with tolerant scorn. And then she cut—the ace of spades. Her grandmother threw up her hands. "Death, I tell you—death—death—death—an' no less."

Gentleman Jim struck the cards out of her hand roughly, and they went flying to all corners of the hut.

"Come outside, Nell—come down to the waterhole, it's cool there, and better fun than listening to an old woman's twaddle. The sun's down now. Come on."

She looked at her grandmother first, partly from habit, but the old woman was still wringing her hands over the danger foretold by the cards, and was blind for the moment to that right under her eyes. So Nellie followed him gladly, only too gladly, down the steep bank to the waterhole. He pushed her down somewhat roughly under the shadow of the western bank, and then flung himself down on the ground beside her, and put his head in her lap. With her little work-hardened hand, she smoothed back his black hair, and he looked up into her face.

"So you love me, Nellie?" he said, somewhat abruptly. "You be sure you love me?"

It was hardly a question, he was too certain of it, and no man should be certain of a woman's love.

She made no answer in words, but the pretty blue eyes smiled down at him so confidingly, that for a moment the man was smitten with remorse. What good would this love ever do her?

"You poor child!" he said. "You poor little girl. I believe you do. Don't do it, Nellie—don't be such a fool."

"Why?" she asked simply.

"Why? Because I shall do you no good."

"But I love you," she whimpered, "an' you won't harm me."

"No, by —— I won't." And for the moment perhaps he meant to keep his oath, for he half rose, as if there and then he would have left her. Perhaps it was too much to expect—all his companions feared him, the outside world hunted him, only this woman believed in him and loved him; and if it is a great thing to be loved, it is a still greater thing to be believed in and trusted. And so when she put her arms around him and drew him back he yielded.

"It is your own fault, Nell, your own fault—don't blame me."

"No," she said, satisfied because he had stayed. "I won't—never." Then she ran her fingers through his hair again.

"I saw a gray hair in the sunshine," she said.

"A gray hair—a dozen—a hundred. My life is calculated to raise a few gray hairs."

"But why—?"

"Why? Why—once on the downward path you can't stop, my dear. However the path has led me to your arms, so common politeness should make me commend the road by which I came."

"You are always good."

"Good! great Heavens! No—only a silly girl would think that. Was I ever good? I'm sure I don't know. If I was a woman soon knocked it out of me."

"A woman! Did you love her?"

"Love her—of course I loved her."

"More 'n you do me?"

"More than I do you!—You're only a little girl—and she—she was a woman of thirty, and she just wound me round her fingers,—her!"

The tears gathered in the girl's eyes—only one thing her simple soul hungered after—she wanted this man's love—she wanted to be allowed to love him in return.

"She didn't love you like me," she said.

"She didn't love me at all, it was I loved her, the young fool. That's the way of the world. Come, Nell, don't cry—that s the bitterness of it. Where's the good of crying? Where's the good of loving me? I wasted all the love I had to give on a woman, who made a plaything of me—oh, about the time you were born I suppose. That's the way of the world, my dear; oh, you 'll learn as you grow older."

"Ben Fisher," said Nellie slowly—"Ben Fisher, Gran says, loves me, an' 'ud marry me. An' he's Macartney's boss man."

The man sprang to his feet and caught her roughly in his arms. He hurt her, but she did not mind; such fierce wooing was better than the indifference which had seemed to mark his manner before. His hot breath was on her face, and in his eyes was an angry gleam, but she read love there too, and was content.

"You, Nellie—you—do you want Ben Fisher? If you go to him—if you have any truck with him—I 'll kill you, Nell."

She closed her eyes and drooped her head on to his shoulder.

"Jes' so," she said, "you can."

"Nell, Nell," called her grandmother's voice from above. "Nell, you come up this minute. Drat the girl, where's she got to? You come along, miss, and help to get supper. There's the bread to set, for Macartney's mob 'll be here early to-morrow."

James Newton held the girl for a moment with a merciless hand.

"Nell, I 'll kill you."

She smiled at him through her tears, then stooped and kissed the hand that held her, and as he loosened his grasp, flew up the embankment and joined her grandmother.

Next day the Durham lads and Gentleman Jim had disappeared. It seemed a wonder in that flat open plain where they could disappear to, but the creek had many windings, and its bed was so wide and so far beneath the surface of the plain, there was ample room for men and horses to hide there.

About three in the afternoon, a lowing of cattle and cracking of stockwhips announced the arrival of Macartney's mob, and the beasts, wild with thirst, for the way had been long and hot, and the waters were dried up for miles back, rushed tumultously down into the waterhole, trampling one another in their eagerness to get to the water. The men could no nothing but look on helplessly, and finally Fisher, a tall young fellow with that sad look on his bearded face, which sometimes comes of much living alone, left the mob to his men, and flinging his reins on his horse's neck went towards the hut.

Nellie stood in the doorway, but when she saw who it was, mindful of her lover's fierce warning of the night before, she drew back into the hut, and the sadness on the man's face deepened, for Nellie Durham, the cattle-duffer's granddaughter, was the desire of his heart, and the light of his eyes, and Murwidgee Waterhole, when he had charge of the cattle, was on the main road to everywhere.

He dismounted and entered, and Mrs. Durham bustled up to him—eager to make amends for Nellie's want of cordiality.

"It's pleased I am to see ye, pleased, pleased," she said, "for 'tis lonesome hereabouts, now the boys is away down Port Philip way."

"Are the boys away?" he asked, watching Nellie, as in obedience to an imperious command from her grandmother, she began to set out a rough meal.

"Oh, ay—there 's on'y Nell an' grandfather, an' me, an' we're gettin' old. Oh, 't is lonesome for the girl whiles."

If it were, she did not seem to feel it, and she steadfastly refused all Fisher's timid advances. Farther away than ever he felt her to-day, and yet she had never looked so fair in his eyes.

He ate his meal slowly, answering the old woman in monosyllables, when she questioned him as to his camp for the night and his movements on the following day. Possibly he may have thought it unwise to take old Durham's wife into his confidence, but if so the men under him were not so reticent, and when they came in a few moments later, chatted freely on their preparations for the night, and half in jest roughly warned the old woman that the cattle must be let alone.

"None o' your larks now, old girl," said Fisher's principal aid. "We mounts guard turn an' turn about, an' the first livin' critter as comes anigh them beasts—the watch he shoots on sight."

"What's comin' anigh 'em?" asked the old woman scornfully. "There's me an' th' old man an' the girl here, an' nary a livin' thing else for miles. They do say," she added, dropping her voice, "the place is haunted. Jackson of Noogabbin was along here a month back, and he told me how the cattle broke camp all along o' the ghost. He seed 'un wi' his own eyes, a great white thing on a trottin' cob it was. Clean through the camp it rode moanin', moanin', an' the cattle just broke like mad."

"Oh, yes—I dessay," said the man, "and when them cattle were mustered, there was a matter o' fifty head missin', I 'll bet. Now if that ghost comes along my way I shall just put a bullet in him sure as my name's Ned Kirton. So there, old lady, put that in your pipe and smoke it. Come along, Nell, my girl—don't be so stingy with that liquor, the old woman 'll make us pay for it, you bet. Why, Nell, I ain't seen such a pretty pair o' eyes this many a long day. Give us just one——"

He had caught her roughly by the shoulder, and bent down to kiss her, but the girl drew back with a low cry that brought Fisher to her aid.

"Let her alone, Ned," he said with a muttered oath.

"Right you are, boss," laughed the other. "There 's a darned sight too much milk and water there for my taste; I like 'em with a spice o' the devil in 'em, I do. But if that 's your taste—well, fair's fair an' hands off, says I."

"It ain't much good, boss," said another man. "She's Gentleman Jim's gal, she is, and I shouldn't sleep easy if I so much as looked at her."

"Gentleman Jim," he repeated, and the bitterness in his heart none of his comrades guessed. "Gentleman Jim I heard of yesterday, somewhere about the head waters of the Murray—no danger from him."

Bill, being a cattle man, cleared his throat and his brain by a good string of oaths—resonant oaths worthy of a man from the back blocks—and then gave it as his opinion that Gentleman Jim's being seen among the ranges yesterday, was no guarantee that he would not be lifting cattle far on the plains to-day.

"Not our cattle," said Fisher grimly. "We set a watch, and the first thing—man or beast, or ghost—that comes down among the cattle, we shoot on sight. D'ye hear that, mother?" and he turned to the old woman, who merely shook her head and groaned.

"It's old I am—old—old—old. It isn't the likes o' us as 'll touch yer beasts."

And Nellie slipped outside the door, and looked wistfully and anxiously across the plain, at the cattle now peacefully grazing on the salt-bush, and at the mocking mirage in the far distance. Never before, it seemed to her, had so much fuss been made about the cattle. The ghost trick had stood them in good stead for some time, and now apparently these men saw through it.

Two ideas she had firmly grasped. Ben Fisher was a man of his word, and Ben Fisher was a good shot.

Her brothers and her lover were down in the creek bed. One of the four would ride through the sleeping cattle to-night and that man would pay for his temerity with his life. The casual mention of her own name with that of the outlaw had sealed his fate. She was as sure of that as she was sure that the sun would set to-night in the west and would rise again to-morrow in the east. It did not occur to her simple soul to inquire the reason why; only she felt that it was so, and her heart was full of one passionate prayer, that the man who rode forth on that perilous errand should not be her lover. Her brothers were dear to her naturally, but her nearest and her dearest were as nothing when weighed in the scale with the love she bore this stranger. He must be saved at any cost—he must, he must. She walked slowly along with down-bent head, till she stood on the top of the bank overlooking the waterhole, and then, hearing footsteps behind her, looked up quickly to see Ben Fisher standing beside her.

"Nellie," he said awkwardly, "Nellie, I—I—mean did that brute hurt you?"

"What? Oh, Ned Kirton. Oh, it's no matter."

"It's dull here for you, Nell, out on the plains, isn't it?" he asked still more awkwardly.

If her heart was full of another man, his was full of a strong man's longing for her.

He saw her position, he knew her helplessness, he felt how much she stood in need of care and guardianship. If she would only give him the right to care for her. His very eagerness made him stupid and awkward, and she, looking up at him in the hot afternoon sunlight, read none of his thoughts, and only saw in him the man who held her lover's life in his hands and would mercilessly take it.

She answered his question sullenly with a shrug of her shoulders.

"No, no."

"But Nellie—oh, Nellie, Nellie—poor little girl, don't you see that—that—"

"What?" she asked, for even she, indifferent as she was, could not fail to see that the man was shaken by strong emotion. "I 'm all right."

"All right, with a devil like that after you, a brute who—Nellie, Nellie, for God's sake give me the right to take care of you."

She looked at him stupidly and then a light dawned on her.

"Do you mean Jim?" she said. "Why, Jim—" and for a moment a tender smile broke about her lips, and a light was in her eyes such as would never be there for the man beside her.

"Oh, Nellie," he groaned, "am I too late after all? I only want to take care of you, Nellie—only to take care of you."

He stepped forward and caught her hands, holding them fiercely as Jim Newton himself might have done.

"Nellie, if you won't let me do anything else, let me help you; for your own sake let me help you."

Clearly outlined they stood against the summer sky; if there should be anybody in the creek-bed, lurking among the rushes and scrub round the waterhole, they would be plainly visible to him. Their attitudes were significant, and their speech was inaudible. If Jim should be there, thought Nellie, and then dismissed the thought. Rash as he was, he would never be so foolhardy as that. And yet she might have noticed a slight movement among the reeds—might have remembered that Gentleman Jim found no companionship in her brothers, and would be pretty sure to find his way to the water-hole at any risk, if it were only to vary the monotony and to see how the land lay. And so after one vain effort to free her hands, she stood still and listened, while Fisher poured into her unwilling, uncomprehending ears the story of his love for her, and then, since that made no impression, he warned her again and again against Gentleman Jim. Foolishly warned her—for was ever woman yet warned against the man she loved. An angry gleam flashed into Nellie's eyes, and she stamped her feet and strove to draw away her hands again.

"I hate you—I hate you. He is good, I tell you—good—good—good! He loves me an'"—oh, the unanswerable argument all the world over—"I love him."

Fisher dropped her hands.

"Oh Nell! Nell! My God! it is too hard."

She looked at him wonderingly, and a dawning pity softened her face. It had never occurred to her that this man could feel any pain. She read it in his haggard face now, and because she was pitiful of all things she put her hand on his arm and said gently, "Poor Ben, I 'm sorry."

It was too much—Fisher had stood her coldness, had heeded not her anger—but the pretty, wistful face looking up so pitifully into his was too much for him. He could resist temptation no longer, he caught her in his arms and smothered her with kisses. Clearly it was marked against the sky, clearly the man crouching among the reeds saw it, and put his own interpretation upon it, and that one passionate embrace sealed Nellie Durham's fate. Well might the cards prophesy disaster and death, for as he slunk away back to his ambush a mile further down, with raging hate at his heart, he swore revenge against the girl who was trifling with him, swore it and meant to keep his oath.

Nellie with an inarticulate cry freed herself and ran towards the hut, and Fisher flung himself face downwards on the crisp dry salt-bush. He had lost everything now he realised, she would not even accord him pity.

And Nellie up at the hut was trying to make her grandmother understand that all chance of the ghost trick being played again with success was out of the question. Not only would it be a failure, but the man who rode through the cattle rode at the risk of his life. But the old woman could not or would not see it.

"Let 'un alone, Nell, let 'un alone—a parcel of women ain't wanted meddlin' wi' the men-folks' business."

"But, Gran—" the girl was wild with anxiety, and trembling with excitement, and the old woman shut her up sharply. She did not choose to hear any more about it, and turned a deaf ear on purpose. Like Nellie she too was of opinion that Gentleman Jim would play the ghost, and if—through no fault of hers— he came to grief, she felt she would not grieve unduly. Nellie's infatuation for him was undeniable, and with a good decent man like Ben Fisher ready to take her it was unpardonable. Nellie had always been soft and yielding to her, once this man were out of the way she would be so again, and the old woman had seen enough of the seamy side of life to desire better things for the helpless girl. So she turned a deaf ear to her anxious warnings; not by word or sign would she interfere. Let be, let be, it should be fate—it should be no doing of hers. Nellie gave up the struggle at last and taking up her favourite position on the doorstep, with her chin in her hands and her elbows on her knees, stared out moodily across the plains, seeking in her brain some way to help. It was not possible to go near them by daylight, the risk of detection was too great, she must wait till it was dark. Fisher crossed her path once, and for a moment a wild thought crossed her brain—to confide her trouble to him—to ask him to have mercy, but she dismissed it as soon as it was born. Betray her lover and then ask his rival to spare him! It was out of the question; she must find some other way. She thought and thought, till for very weariness she closed her eyes, and slept with her head against the door-post. The long level beams of the setting sun made a golden glory of her hair and seemed to be striving to smooth out the look of care and pain, which was already marked on the fair young face. Ben Fisher passed and paused.

"Pretty, ain't she?" said the old woman; "a dainty mossel for any man."

"Ay," said Fisher quietly, "ay," and passed on, wondering to himself, as many another man has done before him—why this girl was so priceless in his eyes—and why, seeing that she was so, he might not have her rather than this reckless outlaw, who would make her the toy of his idle hours, and when she became a burden to him throw her aside, like a worn-out horse or a dog he had no further use for.

He bit his lip and clenched his hands, and the men when he gave the orders for the night, muttered to one another that the boss meant business an' no mistake. "Ghost or no ghost. 'T wouldn't be much good anybody meddlin' wi' the cattle now. He was mighty struck on the gal, he was—but it didn't seem to be interfering wi' business nohow."

He was mighty struck on the girl, and his thoughts were so full of her that sleep seemed out of the question, so he took the first watch with Ned Kirton for his mate.

Out on the plains here, had they been quite certain of the honesty of the Durhams, one man would have been quite sufficient to mount guard, his duties being simply to ride round the cattle, and should any seem restless or inclined to roam to head them back again. Even as it was, two seemed an almost unnecessary waste of energy, more especially as the other men were camped close by, ready to spring to their feet at a moment's call.

It was a still, hot night; the moon, though not near full, still shed a sufficient light to distinguish everything quite plainly; the men's camp, the sleeping cattle, the hut and outbuildings a little to the left, so calm and peaceful.

Fisher, as he sat on his motionless horse, began to think one guard was more than enough, and to speculate as to whether he should not tell Kirton to go to sleep and leave the cattle to him. Sleep was not likely to come to him, he thought, with that haunting girl's face ever before his eyes. He turned his horse so that he should not see the hut, and then found himself riding round the camp, in order to bring it into view again.

"It's all right, boss," said Kirton, as he passed. "Things is as quiet as quiet. Ghosts ain't expected to walk before twelve though, are they?"

Fisher laughed. "No," he said, "but somehow I don't believe the ghost intends to trouble us after all. They 're scared at our preparations. I think one man 'll do after midnight."

He rode on a little way, when suddenly something induced him to turn his head, and he saw distinctly, in the moonlight, a white figure come out of the hut and make its way quickly in the direction of the creek. It was a woman's figure, with a kerchief across the head, but whether it was Nell or her grandmother he could not at that distance or in that light say.

He rode up to his mate quickly.

"There's some mischief brewing, Ned," he said, looking towards the figure, which had apparently changed its mind, and was now walking in a direction which would bring it to the banks of the creek, a little beyond the cattle camp. "You waken the boys quietly, and tell 'em to be on the look out, and I 'll follow the old woman and see if I can't circumvent her little tricks."

"It ain't the old woman," said Kirton, "it's the gal."

"You be hanged," said Fisher, who preferred Mrs. Durham should get the credit for any midnight escapades. "It's the old harridan herself, and I 'll keep my eye on her."

He slipped to the ground, tied his reins to the stirrup, and the old stock horse, understanding the situation, stood quietly, while his master quickly and quietly followed in the footsteps of the girl, for it was Nellie; he was sure of that when she came abreast of the camp. She was evidently terribly hurried, and hardly seemed to notice the men and cattle as she passed. In truth Nellie did not, for her grandmother had kept so careful an eye on her, she had been unable to leave the hut until she was asleep, and now it was so late, she dared not take the longer and safer way round by the windings of the creek, lest her lover should have already started on his perilous ride. Whether she thought the men would not notice her or whether she hardly cared if they did, Fisher never knew. She held a cloth closely over her head and never turned to the right or left, though he thought his footsteps must be clearly audible as he tramped in his long riding boots over the crisp dry salt-bush.

Truth to tell, Nellie heard nothing save the beating of her own heart. It was such a desperate venture, she was afraid of her grandmother, she was afraid of Ben Fisher, she was afraid even of the man she was trying to save, but most of all she was afraid of being too late, and so the poor child went on, her heart full of one passionate, unspoken prayer, that she might be in time to save him. It was little wonder then that she never turned her head, never heard the footsteps so close behind her. She reached the brink of the creek at length and peered into its depths, then turned and skirted along the top of the bank, Fisher following closely in her track.

They had gone but a little way when he saw, greatly to his astonishment, that the bank, instead of being a steep drop of about twenty feet, gently sloped like it did near the hut, and a track, half hidden by thick scrub, ran down the slope. Down this track the girl went swiftly, her skirts raising a little whirl of dust behind her. The man paused a moment, and by the light of the moon examined his pistols to see they were loaded, for he judged he was doing an unwise thing. Should there be men there, as he more than half suspected, there was no knowing what might happen; but still he never thought of turning back, that Nellie was there was more than sufficient reason he should follow. When he looked again he was startled to find she had vanished, and the measured sound of a horse's hoof-beats broke on his ear. At the same moment he saw the path took a turn in the scrub, and drawing out a pistol, ran down it. As he turned the corner, he came full on Nellie standing motionless in the moon-light; the covering had fallen from her head, and she was stretching out her arms to a mounted figure which was draped, horse and all, in a long white cloth which fell almost to the ground.

It flashed across the overseer that this was the "Trotting Cob," this was the ghost he had been warned against, and a very substantial, life-like ghost it was too. He wondered as he stood there that any man could be deceived.

The girl stood right in its path, right between the two men, and to move, the horseman must either ride over her or turn into the scrub.

He seemed inclined to do neither, but with an angry oath flung back the covering from his face.

"You, girl!" he said.

Then she burst out, half-sobbing, "Oh, Jim, Jim! I was afraid I 'd be too late. Oh, Jim, Gran wouldn't let—"

"Too late!" said the man; he spoke apparently with an effort, but in such grave, cultured tones that Fisher, who was a man of but little education, himself stood silent with wonder. "Too early, I think. I told you how it would be, Nell. I believed in you, Nell, so help me God, I did, but I saw you this afternoon with that man, and now you have betrayed me. You will have it

- 14 -

then," and before Fisher could stop him or shield her, he had drawn a pistol from his belt and shot her in the breast. So close she was there was not a chance of missing, and she fell backwards and lay there in the dusty track, the pale moonlight lighting up her fair hair, and the dark stain widening, widening, on the bosom of her dress.

Fisher's first thought was for vengeance, but his hand shook and his shot flew wide, and the other man, apparently giving no heed to him, flung himself from his saddle on to the ground beside the girl.

"Oh, Nell, Nell, little girl, and I trusted you."

She put her little bloodstained hand on his arm, and smiled up into his face with such a world of love in the dying eyes, that Fisher looking on dared not for very pity mar her last moments by word or sigh.

Time enough when she was gone, for the two men to settle accounts.

"Jes' so," she gasped, her one idea strong in death; "I was—near, too late—don'—go—nigh the camp. Ben Fisher—will—shoot the ghost—on—sight."

"But—but—"

Pity for the girl, dying misjudged by the hand she loved, impelled Fisher to speak.

How great had been his share in the tragedy he hardly as yet realized; that would come later.

"It wasn't her fault this afternoon," he said roughly; "it was mine, and this evening she never knew I followed her."

"Oh, my God—my little girl, my poor little girl."

He lifted her up in his arms and made a half effort to staunch the wound, but she was evidently dying fast—past all human aid.

"Jim—you—won't—go—anigh—the—camp?"

"Nellie, Nellie, don't die, my darling—don't leave me; don't let me have this on my conscience. I love you, Nellie—you are all there is to live for. I love you."

"Better 'n *her*?" she gasped.

He looked down at her in wonder, then covered the white face with kisses.

"Better a thousand times—better than any woman that ever lived. Forgive me, Nell, forgive me."

She was going fast, but she understood him, and the man looking on saw peace and happiness on her face.

"I love you, Jim."

"There never was a daughter of Eve, but once ere the tale of her years be done,

Shall know the scent of the Eden rose—but once beneath the sun!

Though the years may bring her joy or pain, fame, sorrow, or sacrifice,

The hour that brought her the scent of the Rose—she lived it in Paradise!"

The horse's hoof-beats kept time to the rhythm of the song. "The hour that brought her the scent of the Rose—she lived it in Paradise!"

"An' I guess," said the driver's voice—breaking in on my reverie—"that's about all there is to tell. Them's the lights of Wongonilla over there. The rest of the story—Lord bless you, it all 'us ended where the gal died. The men I guess did'nt feel much inclined for fighting after that. Anyhow I b'lieve Ben Fisher came back dazed like to camp an' told 'em what 'd happened. But though they scoured the country, Gentleman Jim got clean away. Fisher? Oh, he weren't no account after it, I b'lieve—gave him a sort a' shock, same as if he 'd killed her hisself. He was speared by the blacks on the Lachlan three years later, they say. He never took up with another gal. The other? Lord, yes—he did—Woa, mare, will you? She's a bit tired, you see—we 've come the pace. Yes, it was all along o' a woman Jim Newton was taken—wanted for a bushranging job, over on the Queensland border—that was fifteen years after. I 've heard my father tell the story. He was one of the troopers that took him, and it was a gal that sold him. Mighty set on her he was. She? Oh, she was gone on another man. A woman's only gone like that once in a way, ye see, an' then, Lord! she is a fool—same as Nellie Durham, an' she was a mighty fool all through, for Fisher was a decent sort of a chap—while the other fellow was an' out-an'-out blaggard. But ye see, if there's a ghost at all, it 's the gal that walks, though they call the place Trotting Cob, and Trotting Cob it'll be till the end of the chapter."

CHRISTMAS EVE AT WARWINGIE

It was a comfortable place, the wide verandah at Warwingie, a place much used by the Warners on all occasions, save during the heat of the day—but the long hot day was drawing to a close now. Slowly the sun was sinking over the forest-clad hills. The heat haze which had hung all day over the eastern outlet to the gully cleared, the faraway blue ranges grew more distinct, and the creeper-covered verandah was once more a pleasant place to lounge in. From the untidy, half-reclaimed garden, came the sound of children's voices, subdued by the distance, and the gentle lowing of the milkers in the stockyard behind the house. But no one came on to the verandah to disturb Tom Hollis and Bessie Warner, the eldest daughter of the house—perhaps they knew better—and yet these two did not seem to have much to say to each other. He leaned discontentedly against one of the posts, moodily staring out into the blue distance, and every now and again flicking his riding boot with his whip; but she looked happy enough as she swung herself slowly backwards and forwards in a rocking-chair, her hands clasped behind her head. Such a pretty girl, oh, such a pretty girl, she was—so dainty and pink and white. Her rosy lips were just parted in a smile; the long, level beams of the setting sun, falling on her through the passion vine, lingered lovingly in her golden hair, and made a delicate tracery as of fine lace work, on her pink gingham gown. Such a pretty picture she made, rocking slowly backwards and forwards, thought her companion, but he dared not say so. And then too it was so hot and so still it was hardly wonderful they were silent.

Silence seemed more in keeping with the quiet evening. They could not agree, and yet they could not quarrel openly. He brought his eyes back from the hills at length to the girl's fair face.

"Oh, Bessie," he said almost in a whisper, "oh, Bessie—"

"Now, Tom," she interrupted, "now, Tom, do be quiet; whatever is the good of going all over it again?"

"If you could only like me a little," he sighed miserably.

"Like you a little! I have liked you a good deal more than a little all my life—but there's where it is. I know you a great deal too well. I like you, oh yes, I believe I may say I love you quite as well even as my own brothers, but—marry you, no thank you. I have lived all my life up here at Warwingie, up among the hills, and I 'm just tired of the monotony of it. Nothing ever happens, nothing ever will happen, I suppose; it's most horribly unexciting; but anyhow I don't see I 'd better matters by going and living alone with you at Tuppoo, even if you 'd take me on such terms, which, of course, you wouldn't."

"You know I would," he said drearily.

"Don't be so foolish, Tom Hollis," said Bessie sharply, rocking away faster than ever. "You know you wouldn't do any such thing. You 'd despise yourself if you did. Why don't you despise me?—I'm sure I 'm showing myself in an extremely disagreeable light for your benefit."

"But I know you, you see. I know you so thoroughly," he said; "and I'd give—I'd give—"

"There, for goodness' sake, stop, and let's hear no more of it. I can't and won't marry you—it 'd be too slow. I don't want to live on the other side of the ranges all the rest of my life. If I 've got to live here at all, this is the nicest side, and I 've Lydia and the children for company, to say nothing of papa and the boys—besides, you 'll come over sometimes."

"I shan't," he said, sullenly, "I shan't. If you don't take me, I 'll not come here to be made a fool of. I shan't come again."

"Don't talk nonsense," she said calmly; "you will; you 'll forget all this rubbish, and be my own dear old Tom again. I should miss you so dreadfully if I didn't see you three or four times a week."

A gleam of hope flashed into his sad brown eyes, and passionate words of love and tenderness trembled on his lips, but, for once in his love-making, he was wise, and turning, gazed silently down the gully again. She would miss him—very well then, she should; he would go away, and not come back for a month at least. The only fear was lest in the meantime some one else might not woo and win her. Those brothers of hers were always bringing some fellow to the house. However—

A bell inside rang furiously, and five boys and girls, ranging between the ages of twelve and three, came racing in from all corners of the garden. Bessie rose from her chair, and shook out her skirts.

"That's tea," she said; "you won't mind a nursery tea with the children, will you? Lydia and I always have it when papa's away. The Campbell girls are here too. Harry, you know, is very much in love with Dora, and, like a good sister, I 'm helping on the match. Aren't you coming?"

He had intended to decline, but she put her hand on his arm in the old familiar way, and he weakly gave in.

"Aren't you dull, all you women alone?" he asked.

"No, sir, of course not; besides, they 'll all be home to-morrow for Christmas."

"They 've at Kara, aren't they?"

"Yes, that bothering old Wilson always has a muster at the most inconvenient times. They want to be home, of course, so they Ve taken every man on the place to help. Dick, at the mature age of ten, is our sole male protector."

"They can be back to-morrow, though?"

"Oh, yes; they Ve bound to be here pretty early too. It's Christmas Day, you know—at least—. Why, what was that?"

She paused on the doorstep and listened.

"Some one coming into the yard," said Hollis. "They must have got away earlier than they expected."

"No—they—."

A sharp cry—an exclamation of fear and terror, and men's voices raised, loud and peremptory.

"That's not—" began Bessie, but Hollis pushed past her into the house. It was a bush house built in the usual primitive style of bush architecture, with all the rooms opening one into the other and dispensing with passages altogether. The dining-room, a big sparsely furnished room, had doors both front and back, and looked on the yard behind as well as on the garden. The table was laid for a substantial tea. Mrs. Warner, Bessie's stepmother, a good-looking woman of thirty, was at the head of the table with the tea-pot in her hand, but the children had left their places and clustered round her; two other girls of sixteen and eighteen were clinging to one another in a corner, and two women servants, raw Irish emigrants, were peering curiously out into the yard, where half a dozen horses and men were now standing. The cook, an old assigned servant, had taken in the situation at once, had made for the dining-room followed by the other two, and was now sitting in the arm-chair, her apron over her head, beating the ground with her feet.

Hollis saw it all at a glance—the big dining-room, the frightened women, the silent children, the sunlit yard beyond, the horses hitched to the post and rail fence, the half dozen bearded blackguardly men, with pistols and knives in their belts—noted it all, even to the blue and white draped cradle in the corner of the room, and the motes dancing in the sunbeams that poured in through the end windows—noted it all, and looked down on the girl at his side.

"Oh, my God!" he muttered, "it's the Mopoke's gang, and—."

He was unarmed, but he looked round vaguely for a second. Two of the men stepped into the doorway and covered him with their pistols.

"Bail up, you ———," said the shorter of the two, a man in a dirty red shirt and torn straw hat, who was evidently the leader of the party, "bail up; throw up your hands, or—," and he added such a string of vile oaths that Bessie, shuddering, covered her face with her hands. Hollis did not at once obey, and in a second a shot rang out and his right hand fell helpless at his side—shot through the wrist.

"If the gent prefers to keep 'em down, I 'm sure we 're alius ready to oblige," said the little man, with grim pleasantry, interlarding his speech with a variety of choice epithets. "Now then, mate, back you steps agin that wall—and Bill," to the other man, "you just let daylight in if he so much as stirs a finger."

Hollis leaned up against the wall, stunned for a moment, for the bullet had smashed one of the bones of his wrist, and torn a gaping wound from which the blood was trickling down his fingers on to the carpet, but with the armed bushranger in front of him he realized the utter hopelessness of his position. Help himself he could not, but he never thought of himself, he never thought even of the other helpless women and children; his heart had only room for one thought—Bessie, pretty dainty Bessie, the belle of the country side. How would she fare at the hands of ruffians like these? He would die for her gladly, gladly, but his death could be of no avail. The men had come in now, and he scanned them one by one, brutal, cruel, convict faces, sullen and lowering; the only one that showed signs of good humour was that of the leader of the band, and his good humour was the more terrible as it seemed to prove how certain he was of them and how utterly they were in his power.

"You will kindly all stand round the room, with your backs to the wall, so I can take a good look at you, an' you can impress my 'aughty features on your minds—kids an' all, back you go. I 'm sorry to inconvenience you, Mrs. Warner, but you must just let the babby cry a bit. I can't have you a-movin about a-obstructin' my men in the execution of their dooty."

The baby in the cradle had wakened up at the shot, had cried uneasily, and now not having been noticed was wailing pitifully, but its mother dared not move. She stood by the window, the two youngest children hanging on to her skirts, a strong-minded, capable woman, who had all her wits about her, but she too saw clearly they were caught in a trap. She looked across at Hollis, but he could only shake his head. There was nothing to be done, nothing.

A man stood on guard at each door, while the other four went through the house; they could hear them yelling and shouting to one another, pulling the furniture about, and every now and then firing off a shot in simple devilment, as if to show their prisoners that they had made sure of their prey and feared no interruption. The baby cried on, and the sunshine stole gradually up the wall; up and up it crept to the ceiling, and the clock ticked noisily on the mantelshelf—but there was no change, no hope for them. A crash of broken wood and glass told them that the bushrangers had found the store-room, and had made short work of bolts and bars. There were spirits stored there, brandy in plenty, as Bessie and her stepmother knew full well, and Hollis scanning their faces read clearly their thoughts—what chance would they have once these men began to drink! Ghastly stories of the bushranging days of Van Diemen's Land rose before him, of innocent children murdered, of helpless women, and a groan burst from his lips as he thought that the woman he loved was in the power of men like these.

Bessie started forward, though the man at the door pointed his pistol straight at her.

"Oh, Tom," she cried, "oh, Tom!"

"You go back," ordered the guard angrily.

"Don't be so hard," said Bessie, suddenly. "You've got us safe enough. What can a lot of women and a wounded man do against you? You look kind," she added, "do let me give baby to his mother, it's wearying to everybody to hear him crying like that, and let me bind up Mr. Hollis's hand, oh, please do."

Her voice trembled at first, but she gained courage as she went on. She looked the man straight in the face, and she was very pretty.

He told her so with a coarse oath that sent the shamed blood to her face, and then crossed the room and spoke to the other man.

They whispered for a moment, and then curtly told the woman they intended to hold Hollis surety for them. If any one attempted to escape, they would, they said, "take it out of his skin." Then one rejoined his comrades, while the other lolled against the doorpost, his pistol in his hand.

Lydia Warner crossed the room and gathered her baby in her arms, and Bessie stepped to Hollis's side.

"Oh, Tom," she whispered, "oh, Tom—" "Hush, dear, hush—here they come." They came trooping in with coarse jokes and rough horseplay, bearing with them spoils from Lydia Warner's well-filled storeroom, among them an unopened case of battle-axe brandy. This was the centre of attraction. For a moment even the man on guard craned his neck to watch, as the leader of the gang, the man they called the Mopoke, produced a chisel and a hammer and proceeded to open it.

Their prisoners took the opportunity to whisper together, Mrs. Warner joining her stepdaughter and Hollis.

"What can we do, Tom, oh, what can we do? They are beginning to drink now, and—"

"Slip away if you can, you and Bessie." "No, no, they will shoot you—besides, we can't."

Bessie was binding up his wrist, and Mrs. Warner, bending over it, seemed to be giving her advice. The bushrangers had opened the case and were knocking off the heads of the bottles and drinking the brandy out of tea-cups, but the Mopoke looked over his shoulder almost as if he had heard them, and briefly reminded them that he held Hollis responsible, and that if any of them "sneaked off" he 'd shoot Hollis "an' make no bones about it, for we ain't a-come here to be lagged."

"Nevertheless," muttered Hollis, "one of you must go—Bessie, I think. They'll be mad with drink soon, and once drink's in them there's no knowing what they 'll do to any of us—go, dear, go—"

"I can't, I can't." The girl's hands were trembling, as she bound her handkerchief round his wrist, and the tears were in her eyes. Creep away to safety and leave him to die—how could she!

He said again, "Go, Bessie, go, they'll never miss you; it's really our only chance—you don't know what they'll do by and by."

"Lydia, you go." Bessie slipped her hand into Hollis's uninjured one and held it tight. Even in his anxiety and misery he felt in her clasp, he read in her eyes, a something that had not been there half an hour ago. Oh, to be safe once more, to be free to woo and win her.

"I can't leave the children," said Mrs. Warner; "the Campbell girls are no good, and besides, Tom wants you to go, don't you, Tom?"

He nodded. It was true enough; he was wild with anxiety to get her away. He would risk his life gladly—thankfully lay it down, if only he could be assured that Bessie was across the ranges safe in the Commissioner's camp at Tin-pot Gully, and for the other women, their danger would be the same whether she went or stayed.

Bessie clasped his hand tighter and leaned her face against his arm for one brief second, while her stepmother went on.

"As soon as it's dark slip out, and I must try and keep them amused. Dora can sing a little and I can play. Go straight across the ranges, and if—and if—I mean, tell your father. Oh, Bessie dear, make haste."

She left them and joined the others, pausing a moment like a brave woman to speak to the leader of the band, and so give Bessie a chance of a last word with Hollis.

The sun had gone down now and darkness had fallen. The room was wrapped in gloom, and Bessie mechanically watched her stepmother draw down the blinds and light a couple of candles on the table, which, while they illuminated the circle of bushrangers, only threw into deeper darkness the corners of the room.

"You will go, dear," muttered Hollis, "if only for the sake of that plucky woman."

"I will do what you tell me," she whispered. "I can't bear to leave you, Tom; if they should find out they will kill you. Oh, Tom, Tom!"

"They won't find out," he said soothingly. "They haven't counted you, nor noticed you much yet. And Mrs. Warner is wonderfully plucky. You ought to try and save her and those girls. Bessie, you don't know what fiends those men can be."

"Yes I do," she said, and he felt her hand tremble; "that is why I don't want to anger them. They have made you responsible, and I 'm afraid—I 'm afraid to leave. Don't you think they 'll go in an hour or two—just take what they want and go?"

"No, I don't," he said. "They are in for a drinking bout now, and God knows what they'll do before it's ended. Darling, for your own sake—for the sake of the others, for my sake, even—you must risk it and get away if you can. We ought to have help before midnight."

"Bessie," said Mrs. Warner, "come and help me to put the two little ones to bed. Mr.—I beg his pardon—Captain Mopoke says he doesn't mind."

"None of your larks now, missis," said the Mopoke; "you jest mind what yer about, or I 'll let daylight into yer gallant defender there."

"That's the way," whispered Hollis tenderly; "go now—go, dear."

She lifted his hand to her breast in the obscurity, and stooping, laid her face against it.

"My darling," he said passionately, "God bless you, my darling; it will be all right, I know. And remember, dear—you won't be angry—remember, I have loved you so. I think I have always loved you, Bessie."

The men round the table were in high good humour, joking with each other and the two Irish servants, who were beginning to think that being "stuck up" was not so terrible after all, while the cook took her apron from her face and joined in the chaff. Hollis was thankful for it. It enabled him to say what he had to say unobserved, for even his guard, feeling sure of him, gave more heed to his comrades' sayings and doings. His broken wrist made him feel sick and faint, and it was only by a strong effort of will he kept his senses at all. If only he could see Bessie safe out of it!

"Go, dear," he whispered again, "go to Mrs. Warner."

"Tom," she whispered, her face still against his hand, "I love you, Tom. I did not know it this afternoon, but I do now. I love you, I love you."

"Bessie!" Mrs. Warner's voice sounded imperative. "Are you never coming?"

"God bless you, my darling!"

He pushed her gently from him, but at the bedroom door, where her stepmother stood waiting for her, she looked back into the dimly-lighted room. The light from the two candles shone on the bushrangers' faces, gleamed on the pistol barrels in their belts, on the dainty china, the glass, and the silver, but all the rest of the room was in gloom. She knew the other women were there, knew the children were there—they were dimly discernible in the corners. She could even see Hollis, but when she looked again the candles stretched out in long beams which reached her eyes and blinded her, and she turned to wipe away her tears.

"Now then, Bessie," said her stepmother, "go, dear—quick, quick. You'll never be missed in the dark, and I 'll light plenty of candles now, and dazzle the Mopoke. Go, Bessie, go."

There was no time for words. They were very fond of one another, those two—fonder than women in their position often are—and Lydia Warner drew her husband's daughter towards her and kissed her tenderly.

"Everything depends on you, Bessie," she said, with a break in her voice, and then she opened the long French window of her bedroom, and Bessie stepped outside, and the door was softly shut behind her.

It was very dark now, very dark indeed, and very still. Quite plainly she could hear the voices and laughter within, and she stood still on the verandah for a moment to collect her thoughts, and let her eyes get accustomed to the gloom. It was a perfect summer's night, hot and still—not a breath of wind stirred the leaves on the trees. Far away from the reed beds at the bottom of the gully came the mournful wail of the curlews, and the whimper of the dingoes rose over the ranges. Overhead in the velvety sky the stars hung low like points of gold. It was so peaceful, so calm this glorious summer's night, this eve of the great festival which should bring to all men good tidings of peace and joy. Could it possibly be that murder and rapine were abroad on such a night as this? Could it possibly be that those nearest and dearest to her were in deadly danger?

It was seven miles, at the very least, to Tin-pot Gully, or, as it was beginning to be called, Toroke—seven miles round by the road, though it was only three across the ranges. But then she did not know the way across the ranges, the bush was dense and close, there was no track, and she might easily be lost for a week there. The only alternative was the road, and it would take her two hours at least to walk, and what might not happen in two hours? She could dimly see the buildings in the yard now, the stable, the cowshed, her father's office, the men's hut, the post-and-rail fence of the stockyards beyond, with the bushrangers' horses hitched to it all in a row. It struck her forcibly how secure, how safe, they must have felt thus to have left their horses, their only means of escape, alone and unguarded. Should she let them go? Should she drive them away? And then another thought flashed into her mind. Why not make use of one of these horses? Whatever she did must be done quickly, and if only she could ride she might bring help in very little over the hour. In an hour not much harm could happen, surely. Surely they might spend their Christmas yet at Warwingie in peace and happiness. Her father would not return to find his home desolate, and Tom—Tom—but no, she dared not think of Tom. Only this afternoon she had laughed his love to scorn, and now there came back to her his face drawn with pain, but full of love and tenderness and thought for her—the sun-bronzed face with soft brown eyes, giving not one thought to himself, not one thought to the life he was risking for her sake. The danger was lest she should be heard. And then, if they shot him, as she most firmly believed they would, what would her life be worth. Not worth living, thought Bessie Warner, as she stole softly up to the horse nearest the slip panels that led out into the home paddock. She had not been born and bred in the bush for nothing, and if she could once get the horse out of the yard half her troubles would be over.

"Woa, horse," she said softly, putting out her hand and patting his neck, "woa, good horse;" but he started back to the utmost limit of his halter, and showed his fear so plainly that she shrunk back in terror lest the noise of his movements should bring out one of the gang. Trembling she took shelter inside the open stable door, her heart beating so hard it seemed to deafen her. The big chestnut settled down quietly again before she ventured out, and this time she picked out a little dark horse. There was a big, quiet-looking white beside him, but though he stretched out his nose to be patted she rejected him because of his colour. Even in the dim light he was clearly visible across the yard, and his absence would be noted at once, while possibly the darker horse would not be so soon missed. He was fairly quiet as she unfastened the reins, which were buckled round one of the rails in the fence. Then she paused with them in her hand, and the desperateness of the venture nearly overwhelmed her. The night seemed quite light to her now. The outlines of the house were plainly marked against the sky, and all the windows were brilliantly lighted up—evidently Lydia had promptly carried out her intentions. Then a child's cry, loud and shrill, broke on the air, and Bessie started. Woa, good horse, go softly now, for life and death hang on the next few moments. The beating of her own heart nearly choked her—her own light footsteps sounded in her ears like the march of a hundred men, and every moment she expected one of those long windows to open and the bushrangers to come rushing out, for not a regiment of cavalry, it seemed to her, could have made more noise than that solitary horse moving quietly behind her. She kept on the grass as much as possible, but it seemed an age before she had reached the slip-panels. They were down as the bushrangers had left them, and she looked back. No, it was impossible to distinguish anything in the yard. The horses even were one blurred mass; unless they inspected them closely her theft could not be detected. It was so still and so dark—never in her life had she been out at night alone before. The noises frightened her, and the silence was still more terrifying. The cry of the curlews was like a child in pain, and the deep, loud croak of a bullfrog from a water-hole close at hand seemed ominous of disaster. She shrank up close beside the dumb animal for companionship and gave another frightened glance back. Then she pulled herself together—this would never do. For Tom's sake, for Lydia's sake, for the children's sake, but most of all for Tom's sake, she must be brave and cool. If she would save them she must not give way to such vague imaginings. Surely she might venture to mount now. She led the horse up to one of the numerous logs that lay strewn about the paddock, and flinging the off-stirrup to the near side to form a rest for her right foot, she climbed on the log and prepared to mount. Often and often she had ridden so—a man's saddle presented no difficulties; but now to her dismay the horse started back in affright at the first touch of her woman's draperies. If he refused to carry her what should she do? Should she let the horse go? No, that would never do. She made another effort, and at last scrambled into the saddle, how she could not have told herself, but once there she kept her seat, for the black, though he plunged and snorted for a moment, soon settled down into a rough canter towards the main road.

It was not easy going on the run, and even when she reached the road it was not much better, for it was only a bush road, unreclaimed, full of stones and stumps and holes, while the heavy bush on either side made it so dark there was very little chance of seeing the danger. Lucky for the girl she was a good horsewoman. She kept urging her horse on, and he responded gallantly, but more than once he stumbled, and had she not had an excellent seat she must have fallen. But he picked himself up sturdily and pushed on. Good horse, brave horse, it can't be more than four miles now. On either side stood the tall trees dimly outlined against the dark sky, and the Southern Cross—the great constellation of Australasian skies—hung right in front of her. She caught sight of it the moment she turned into the road. It was there every night of the year of course, but looking straight at the golden stars it seemed to Bessie it had been sent to her this Christmas Eve to comfort and encourage her—a sign and a token that all would be well with her and hers.

Then she heard sounds of voices ahead and the gleam of a fire, and she drew rein smartly. No one would she trust, no one dared she trust, save the

Commissioner at Toroke, and who would these people be camped by the roadside? The district had a bad name, the times were troubled, and a helpless woman might well be excused for pausing; but she had no time to waste, she must take all risks, and she brought her reins down smartly across her horse's neck, and he started forward at a gallop. There was a shout and a curse, and she saw three figures start up round the fire, and then she found bullocks rising up all round her, and knew that she had come on a bullock driver's camp. A regular volley of curses burst on her as she scattered the bullocks in all directions, but she dared not stop—how could she trust herself to men like these?—and faster and faster she urged her horse forward. He stumbled more than once in the rough roadway, but at last the sound of voices died away, and looking back the fire was but a bright speck in the darkness. On again, up a steep hill where for very pity's sake she must needs draw rein and let her horse pick his way carefully, up and up, till after what seemed interminable now she found herself on top of the ridge overlooking Tin-pot Gully. The gully was but a narrow cleft among the surrounding ranges, where in winter flowed a creek the banks of which had proved wonderfully rich in gold, and the rush had been proportionately great It had been a pretty creek a year ago, trickling down amidst ferns and creeper-covered rocks, and so lonely that only an occasional boundary rider in search of stray cattle had visited it; but now it was swarming with life, and was reduced to the dull dead level of an ordinary diggers' camp. The tall forest trees had been cut down, and only their blackened stumps were left; the dainty ferns and grasses and creepers had all disappeared before the pick and shovel, and rough windlasses, whips, and heaps of yellow earth marked the claims, while along the banks of the creek, now a mere muddy trickle, stood the implements of the diggers' craft, cradle and tub, and even here and there a puddling machine. The diggers' dwellings, tents and slab-huts, and mere mia-mias of bark and branches, were dotted up the hill-sides wherever they could get a foothold, and of course as close to their claims as possible. There was no method, no order; each man built how he pleased and where he pleased; even the main road wound in and out between the shafts, and its claims to be considered permanent were only just beginning to be recognized.

The Government camp was on a little flattened eminence, overlooking the embryo township. They were all alike, those police camps of early gold-fields days. The flagstaff from which floated the union jack, the emblem of law and order, was planted in such a position as to be plainly visible in the mining camp. Opposite it stood the Commissioner's tents, his office, his sitting-room, his bed tent, his clerk's tent, comfortable and even luxurious for that time and place, for they were as a rule floored with hard wood and lined with baize; just behind was the gold tent, over which the sentries stood guard day and night, and behind it again were the men's quarters and the horses' stables. Down the creek, men of every rank were gathered together from all quarters of the globe; the diggers' camp was untidy, frowsy, and unkempt, but here on the hill the Commissioner reigned, and law and order ruled supreme.

There was a blaze of light from the Miners' Arms—the tumbledown shanty, half of bark and half of canvas, where the diggers assembled every night—and a crowd of men were at the door lustily shouting the chorus of a sea-song. Here was help in plenty, but she dared not trust them, and galloped on across the creek, dry now in the middle of summer, and up the hill again towards the tents of the police camp, which gleamed white against the dark hillside. A sentry started up and challenged her as she passed the gold tent, but she paid no heed, and the next moment she had slipped off her horse and was standing panting and breathless in the open door of the Commissioner's tent. The light from the colza-oil lamps fell full on her white face, on her golden hair streaming over her shoulders, and on her dainty pink gown, somewhat torn and soiled now. Three young men were seated at the dinner-table, two of them in the uniform of Gold Commissioners—the braided undress coat of a cavalry officer—and all three sprang to their feet.

"Oh, Captain Cartwright," she panted, "they have—'stuck up' Warwingie, and they're going to shoot Tom Hollis."

"What?"

But before she had time to explain, one man—she recognized him as the Commissioner from the Indigo Valley on the other side of the ranges—had forced on her a glass of wine, and while Captain Cartwright was shouting orders to his troopers, he drew from her the whole story.

"We 'll have to be careful, Cartwright," he said, when five minutes later they were riding over the ranges at the head of ten stalwart troopers. "It appears Hollis is surety for the lot, but he insisted on Bessie Warner making her escape at all risks. He is a plucky fellow, Hollis, but it was the only thing to do. If they 'd been let alone all night—well, when they're sober I wouldn't trust 'em, and when they 've drunk they 're fiends incarnate. Close up, men, close up a little to the right, sergeant, and we 'll dismount before we come to the stockyards."

They rode across the ranges, and it was not long before the house came into view, ablaze with light, and the troopers crept round it. Then, when they were all assembled, Captain Cartwright with his revolver in his hand stepped on to the verandah and pushed open the door, while Bright, the Commissioner from the Indigo, entered at the other side.

"Bail up, throw up your hands now, or I'll shoot every man jack of you."

It was nearly an hour and a half since Bessie had left, but the bushrangers were still round the table. The dainty china was all smashed and broken, and the men were throwing cups and glasses at one another in very wantonness. There was no one on guard now, and the women were huddled together terrified in one corner, while still against the wall leaned Hollis, exactly where Bessie had left him.

"Hurrah!" he shouted as his glance met the Commissioner's, and hardly had the word left his lips when the Mopoke turned, raised his pistol, and shot him right in the chest. He slipped to the floor with a great singing in his ears, and when he came back to consciousness again young Bright was standing over him holding a glass of brandy to his lips, and Mrs. Warner had her arm beneath his head.

"Better, old chap, eh?" said Bright, cheerily. "The Mopoke made a mistake this time, for Cartwright shot him like a dog, and the others will renew their acquaintance with her Majesty's jails."

"Bessie, Bessie, where is Bessie? If I can only live till she comes!"

"Of course you will. What nonsense Cartwright's going to bring her back with him."

"It's all up with me, old man," he gasped, "I know. But we 've come out much better than I expected, and—and—if I don't see—Bessie—you must tell her—it was worth it. Poor little Bessie, she said—she loved me—it was only a passing fancy—I hope—I think—"

His eyes closed wearily, and Bright touched Mrs. Warner's shoulder.

"Put a pillow under his head," he said, "and—oh, here's Miss Bessie."

No one asked how she had come so soon—only her stepmother silently resigned her place to her. Hollis seemed just conscious of her presence, but he was almost past speech, and they watched him silently. The doctor came, and shook his head.

"A very short time now," he said. Ten o'clock, eleven o'clock; the moon had risen over the hills, the midsummer moon, and all the garden was bathed in the white light. They had opened the windows and drawn up the blinds to give him more air, but it was very near now—very near indeed—only a matter of minutes. The clock on the mantelshelf struck midnight, and he opened his eyes. He could see through the open door right away down the gully, just as he had seen that afternoon.

"How lovely it is," he said.' "Bessie, kiss me, Bessie. I—was that twelve o'clock? It is Christmas Day then. I wish you many happy Christmases, Bessie. Darling—don't you grieve—it was worth it. Good-bye."

LOST

"Helm, old man, we 've lost the track!"

"Don't be a howling idiot, man. Lost! how could we be lost? Why, there's the track right ahead, and pretty fresh too."

But Anderson flung himself off his horse on to the dry crisp grass, and covered his face with his hands.

"I'll tell you," reiterated his mate, leaning forward in his saddle and shading his eyes, "I see hoof-marks quite plain. Why, they might have been made yesterday!"

"They were made yesterday," groaned the other, hopelessly. "Don't you see, my dear fellow, we made them ourselves."

"What!"

Helm raised his head and swore a passionate oath, then sprang from his horse, stooped over the faint track, ran wildly along it for a few yards, turned back, and again cried out that the other was playing some ghastly joke off on him.

"It's too bad, Anderson, too bad. Get up, man, and don't be a fool. Come on, there 's very likely water on the other side of that ridge. You'll feel better after you've had a good drink."

"That's the ridge we passed last night, I tell you. Water—oh, yes, there's water there, but it's as salt as the sea."

"The salt-pan! No, by heaven, no, I won't believe that. That's miles behind us!"

"Nevertheless," said the other man, drearily, "it's the same old salt-pan. You 'll see it the moment we cross the ridge."

"Come on, then, come on. Don't sit groaning there: let's know the worst. I can't believe it, I won't believe it till I see for myself."

"The horses ought to have a spell if we're ever to get out of this," muttered Anderson; but he followed his companion's lead, mounted his tired horse, and rode slowly on after him towards the still distant ridge.

Out back beyond the Mulligan is No Man's Land. They had gone out to seek new country, crossed the Queensland border into South Australia, and now, old bushman as he was, Anderson had only the vaguest idea of their whereabouts. Ever since they started it had been the same trouble; the season had been exceptionally dry, and everywhere the waters were dried up. First one horse had died, then another, until at last they were reduced to only three;

still they had pushed on, for the blacks told a tale of a magnificent waterhole where the water was permanent, and Anderson had a certain amount of faith in the unerring wisdom of the children of the soil where water was concerned. So he pushed on, hoping against hope, till the younger man, more fearful, perhaps more prudent, persuaded him to turn back. But it was too late. The weakest horse, the one they had used as a packhorse, gave in, and had to be left behind the first day of their return journey; and now, on the fourth, they had just made the terrible discovery they were going round on their own tracks. They had been so thankful—so hopeful—when they struck that track in the morning.

Anderson knew there was another party out better appointed than they were; these might be their tracks, and possibly they had water with them. They might even have come across water—and water—water—if only they had a little water. And so they had pushed on, eagerly, hopefully, till the terrible truth began to dawn on the older and more experienced bushman. The weather for the last two days had been dull and cloudy, they had not caught a glimpse of the sun, and hourly they had expected a thunderstorm, which would not only clear the air, but would supply them with the water they needed; but to-day the clouds had all cleared away, and the only effect of their presence had been that they had lost their bearings completely. Where and when they had lost them Anderson could not say even now, and he was loth at first to share his misgivings with his mate; but the sight of the ridge decided him. If they found, as he fully expected to, the salt-pan they had passed the night before on the other side, then most surely were they lost men—lost in a cruel thirsty land where no water was.

He pondered it over in his mind as he rode slowly after his companion. "There was no hope. There could possibly be no hope." Over and over again he said it to himself as a man who hardly realizes his own words—and then they topped the low ridge, and right at his feet lay the salt-pan glittering in the sun.

"Cruel—cruel—cruel!" Helm had flung himself face downwards on the hard ground now, and given way to a paroxysm of despair all the more bitter for his former hopefulness. Anderson looked down on him pityingly for a moment, as one who had no part in his trouble, then he looked away again. Save for the sunshine, it was exactly the same scene, the very same they had looked upon last night—there lay the glittering salt-pan, white as driven snow, above it the hard blue cloudless sky, and all around the dreary plain, broken only by the ridge on which they stood. And yet in different circumstances he might have admired the landscape, for it had a weird beauty all its own; miles and miles he could see in the clear bright atmosphere, far away to the other side of the wide lake, where a dark clump of trees or scrub was apparently raised in the sky high above the horizon. He knew it was only the effect of the mirage, another token, had he needed a token, that there was no moisture, no water, not the faintest chance of a drop of rain. And yet there had been some rain not so very long ago, for the mesembryanthemum growing in dark green patches close to the edge of the salt was all in flower, pink, and red, and brightest yellow, such gorgeous colouring; and by that strange association of ideas, for which who shall account, his thoughts flew back to the last Cup Day, and he saw again the Flemington racecourse, and heard in fancy the shouts of the people as the favourite passed the winning-post, On the ground in front of him were long lines of crows, perched in the stunted boxwood trees above his head, filling the air with their monotonous cawing. He laughed at the mockery of the thing. The other man raised his head.

"Old man, what is it? Is it possible that—"

What wild imaginings for the moment had passed through his brain he could not himself have told; but whatever his hopes might have been, they were gone the moment he looked in his mate's face.

"Man," he said, sharply, "are you mad?"

Anderson was sobered in a second.

"No," he said, bitterly, "but as far as I can see, it must come to that before we 've done."

"No, no, we won't give up hope yet. Is there no hope?"

Anderson sat down beside him, and pointed silently to the horses. If ever poor beasts were done, were at their last gasp, they were, as they stood there, their noses touching the ground. The bushman's slender equipment had been reduced to its scantiest proportions, and yet it seemed cruelty to force them to carry even those slender packs; even the canvas water-bags, dry as tinder now, hanging at their necks, were a heavy burden. Wiser than their masters they had crawled beneath the shade, scanty as it was, of the boxwood trees, and stood there patiently waiting—For what? For death and the pitiless crows patiently waiting overhead.

"Exactly," Helm answered his companion's unspoken thought, "but we can't sit and wait like that. Man, we must try to get out of this at any rate. We cant sit here and wait for the crows."

Anderson sighed heavily.

"What can we do?" he asked. "We must spell a bit. The horses are done. As it is I 'm afraid yours will have to be left and well have to go on foot. There must be water about somewhere, for look at the crows; but we can't find it, and we couldn't have searched more carefully."

"Why not shoot the old horse if he's no good? His blood might—"

"Nonsense, man. Aren't you bushman enough yet to know that drinking blood 's only the beginning of the end? Once we do *that*—"

"Well, after?" asked Helm.

But the other did not answer, for he, too, in his heart, was asking, "After?" And their lips were dry and parched, and their tongues swollen, and before them lay the salt-pan, with right in the centre a little gleam of dark blue water which mocked their misery. There was nothing for it but to lie down beneath the scanty shade and rest. They were too weary to push on, all their energy had departed, and Helm, lying on his back looking up at the patches of blue sky that peeped through the branches, said with a sigh,

"If we 're done for, I wish to heaven the end would come now. I can't stand the thought of—of—What's it like, old man? Is it very bad, do you think?"

"As bad as bad can be."

"And is there no hope?"

What could he say, this man who had lived in the bush all his life? What hope could he give, when practically his experience told him there was no hope— that if they would save themselves from needless pain they would turn their pistols against themselves and die there and at once. But the love of life is strong in us all, and the hope of life is as strong. How could they die, these strong men with life in every vein? No, no, surely it was impossible. An iguana scuttled across in front of them and Helm started up eagerly.

"There," he said, "there—and I never thought. Look at that beast. There must be water somewhere or how could he live."

Anderson sighed.

"Yes, there's the bitterness of it. I know there's water about if only we could find it; but as we didn't find any when we had everything in our favour there's not much good in our wasting time looking now. After all I believe those beasts must live without, though they say they don't. No, old chap, our only hope lies in pushing on to the nearest water we know of."

"Then don't let us lie here wasting precious minutes. Every minute is of consequence; let's make a start. We must push on."

Push on! They had been pushing on ever since they left Yerlo station ten days ago, and this is what it had brought them to.

"It's no good wearing ourselves out in the heat of the day," said Anderson, "wait till evening and we'll do twice as much."

"Which way?"

"South-east, I think. If we can only hold out we ought to fetch Gerring Gerring Water. As far as I know this must be Tamba salt lake, and if so—"

"Karinda's just to the north there."

"A hundred and twenty miles at the very least and not a drop of water the whole way. No, that's out of the question, old man; our only hope lies in reaching Gerring Gerring."

"And you don't see much probability of our doing that?"

"Well, we can try."

He felt a great pity, this older man, for the lad—he called him a lad for all his four-and-twenty years—doomed to die, nay, dying at this very moment, in the prime of his manhood. They could but try, he said over and over again, they could but try.

And then as they rested they fell to talking of other things—talked of their past lives and of their homes as neither, perhaps, had ever talked before.

"My old mother 'll miss me," said Charlie Helm with a sigh, "though Lord knows when she'll ever hear the truth of the matter."

"Umph, I don't know, but I guess if we do peg out, it'll be some considerable time before they can read the store account over us. Have you got any paper about you?"

"Not a scrap. We can leave a message on the salt though."

"It'll be blown away before to-morrow. Who do you want to write to? Your mother? That girl?"

Helm turned his face away. The man had no right to pry into his private concerns.

"Write to your mother, lad, write to your mother by all means. Mothers are made of different clay to other women; but don't you bother about the other. Women are all alike, take my word for it. It's out of sight out of mind with all of them. But write to your mother."

"Some one may pass this way," pondered the younger man, hardly heeding his words. "It's just worth trying," and he lay silent while Anderson talked on or rather thought aloud.

"It's of the boy I'm thinking," he said. "The poor helpless little one. He never throve since his mother died. She didn't go much on me, but the boy was everything to her though he was a cripple. Well—well—if I were only certain he was dead now it wouldn't be half so hard. He'd be better dead, I know, but I couldn't think it before; he was all I had, and the last time I saw him he put up his little hand—such a mite of a hand—and clutched his daddy's beard. He was all I had, how could I wish him dead? But now—now—my God!—if I were certain he was dead and it hadn't hurt much."

Helm sprang to his feet, and swore an oath.

"We're not going to die," he cried, "not as easily as all that. Come on, we have wasted enough precious time.

"Not till it's a little cooler. It's no good, I tell you, wearing ourselves out in the heat."

And Helm, seeing the advice was good, lay down again. Lay down and tried not to listen to the cawing of the crows, the only sound that broke the stillness—tried not to think of cool waters; not to think of a household down south; not to think of the girl who, notwithstanding his mate's cynical warning, filled all his thoughts. He dozed a little and dreamed, and wakened with a start and a strong feeling upon him that it had been something more than a dream, that some one had really called him, was calling him still. Was it his mother's voice, or that girl's, or was it Anderson's? Anderson was sleeping heavily, and strong man as he was, sobbing in his sleep. Helm stretched out a hand to awaken him and then paused. Why should he? What had he better to offer than these broken dreams?

He broke a branch from a tree, thereby scattering the crows and stepped down to the edge of the glittering white salt. It crunched beneath his feet like sand, and he went on till the hard crust began to give way beneath him and the thick mud oozed up. Then when he thought it was moist enough to resist the fierce hot wind, which was blowing from the north like a breath from an oven, he prepared to write his last message. And then came the difficulty.

What was he to say? What could he say? Not that he had so little, but so much. And it might never be read after all, or at best it would only be read by some station hand who, once they were dead, would give but a passing thought to their message, only a passing thought to their sufferings. They had found a skeleton, he remembered, the first year he had been on Yerlo, a skeleton that must have been lying there years, a poor wind-tossed, sunbaked thing from which all semblance of humanity had long since departed, and he, in his carelessness, had thought so little of it, had never realized the awful suffering that must have been before the strong man came to *that*.

And now—and now—he took his stick and wrote in large printed letters on the crisp salt—

STOP. LOST.

"James Anderson and Charles Helm were lost on the 20th October. They have gone S.E. from the salt-pan. Will you kindly send word to Mrs. Helm, The Esplanade, St. Kilda, and to Miss Drysdale, Gipps Street, East Melbourne."

Then he wrote his name, "Charles Helm."

It seemed so feeble, so inadequate, not a hundreth part of what he felt did it express, and yet what could he say? Not even in his extremity could he write tender messages to his loved ones there. They would know, surely they would know, they would understand, that his thoughts had been full of them when he wrote that cold message. What more could he say? But would they ever know the love and longing that had filled his heart? Would his mother ever know that her boy had thought of her at the last? Would Mabel Drysdale understand how he had cared for her?—all he had meant to convey by the mere mention of her name? He stepped slowly back and wakened his companion.

"Mate," he said, "don't you think we'd better be travelling? It's a little cooler now, and it 's getting late."

Anderson struggled to his feet wearily and then went down to the salt-pan.

"So you 've been leaving a last message," he said; "I 'm afraid it's not much good. Who 's likely to pass this way?"

"It's only a chance, of course," said Helm, "but—well—I 'd like them, if possible, to know I 'd thought of them."

"And a woman, too," laughed Anderson cynically, "if we get out of this you 'll learn, I expect, just about how little value she sets on your care for her."

"You 've been unlucky," said the younger man gently; "there are women who—but there, I don't suppose we'll come through. Anyhow, it's time we started.

"Well—well, keep your faith and I'll keep mine. Perhaps here and there, there may be a woman worth caring about, but they 're few and far between."

"Don't you want to say anything?" asked Helm.

"Who? I? No. Who is there to care a straw whether I leave my carcase to the crows or not? There's only the boy, and he's too young to understand. But, I say, you might have mentioned the name of the station," and taking the stick from Helm's hand, he walked out on the salt and wrote;

LOST

"Please let them know at Yerlo," and signed his name, "James Anderson."

"There's my last will and testament," he said. "Come on now."

Helm went up to the horses.

"It's no go," he said. "My poor old beggar's done."

"I expected it, old chap. We'll have to foot it; mine's only a shade better than yours. Clearly we'll have to leave yours behind. Mine can carry the pack a little farther, but I really don't think he can carry me."

It was still very hot, but the shadows of the boxwood trees had grown longer, and there was just a promise of the coming night in the air. They must walk, for they had only the one horse now, and it did not seem likely he could hold out long. The other had lain down to die, and whether this one could crawl on under the slender pack was a question Anderson asked himself more than once. That he could carry either of them was out of the question. They put a blanket or two on his back, their pistols, and the empty waterbags, and then it seemed cruelty to force the poor beast to move, but necessity knows no law, and they started slowly on their hopeless journey round the salt-pan, Anderson leading the way, Helm following with the horse. So slowly they went, and their only hope lay in speed. Helm looked back a little sadly at the dying horse, which had made an effort to rise, as if in mute protest against being left.

"Poor old beggar," he said, "wouldn't it be kinder to put him out of his misery?"

"Oh, give him a chance for his life," said Anderson. "I 've known horses to recover in the most wonderful way. After he 's had a spell he may find water for himself; anyhow, we 'll give him the chance."

It was a blessed relief when the sun sank beneath the horizon; the night was still and hot, but the wind dropped at sundown, and the men found it easier to walk in the dark. The crows had followed them as long as it was day, but they, too, left as soon as the darkness fell. They were unaccustomed to walking, and it would have been hard work under the most favourable circumstances; as it was, it was cruel. They did not talk much, for what had they to say? An hour or two, and the moon rose, a full moon, red and fiery, and as she rose slowly to the zenith, silvering as she rose, the plain grew light as day. Every little stick and stone, every little grass blade, was clearly outlined, the low ridge which they were leaving behind, the ridge where they had found their worst fears realized, loomed large behind them, while the salt-pan to their left stretched away one great lake of glittering white, which it seemed to Helm they could never round.

"How long, Anderson," he asked, "before we can hope to reach the other side?"

"Not before morning, man. I don't see we can do it before morning."

Then they plodded on a little further, neither liking to be the first to give in, though their mouths were parched, and burning thirst was consuming them. But still they walked steadily on till more than half the night was gone; at last Helm flung himself down on the ground.

"I must rest," he said, "if I die for it;" and Anderson sat down quietly beside him.

Then sleep, merciful sleep, came to them in their weariness, and they slept till the first faint streaks of dawn began to appear in the eastern sky. It was a dreary, hopeless waking, the salt lake was behind them now, and all around was the plain, bare hard earth in some places, patches of grass in others, not a living thing visible, even the crows had gone, and, though the foul birds had filled Helm with a shrinking horror, their absence was still more terrible, for did it not show that they were plunging farther and farther into the desert, farther and farther from the water without which they could not live out another day. The sun rose higher and higher, till the full force of his rays seemed more than they could bear, and yet the nearest shade was miles away, a line of trees or scrub dim on the horizon.

Neither mentioned the significance of the absence of the crows, though both were thinking of it, but at last Helm said,

"The trees, let's go for the trees. This is past bearing."

But Anderson shook his head.

"They 're clean out of the way, man," he said sadly. "Try to hold out a little longer. The old horse is keeping up wonderfully. I never thought he 'd hold out so long."

"He's very nearly at his last gasp," said Helm, and they relapsed into silence again.

On, and on, and on, the thirst was so bad now they could hardly speak to one another, still they pushed on under the burning rays of the almost vertical sun, every step it seemed must be their last. Was it really only last night they discovered they were lost, only last night? Another mile, and another, and the heat grew unbearable, and Helm, without a word, turned to the left, and made for the trees. Anderson paused a moment, and then followed him, though to him it was giving up the struggle. If they turned out of the path which led to the only water they knew of, turned into this pathless wilderness, what possible chance was there for them, and yet how could they stand this terrible heat any longer?

"I tell you I shall go mad," moaned Helm. "I didn't think I was a coward, but I can't stand this. Old chap, don't let me go mad; shoot me if you see I 'm going mad."

"Mad," said the other bravely, "nonsense, man, you're all right. You'll feel better presently when you've had a spell."

The lines of trees resolved itself on closer inspection into close-growing gidya scrub, and long before they reached it the crows had again made their appearance. A little flock kept them company, waiting on in front, rushing up behind as if perchance they might be late, wheeling round on either side.

"There must be water there," said Helm eagerly, "look at the crows again."

"Don't build on it, old chap," said the other. "The scrub is too thick for us to find it."

But Helm was not to be dissuaded, and he wasted his energies in a frantic search for water. His mate looked more soberly, because more hopelessly, but the result was the same, and finally they lay down in the shade and slept again, slept soundly too, in spite of the crows, which were more confident, more impudent, than ever. Night fell, and with the darkness grew in Helm an intense desire to be on the way again.

"We 're wasting time," he kept saying hoarsely, for his tongue was so swollen he could hardly speak at all, "wasting time. Don't you see they 'll be expecting us in to supper at Gerring Gerring, and I shouldn't like the crows to get there first. They might frighten her, you know, she's only a girl and she hasn't seen so much of them as you and me. Those knowing old crows! they 're not here now. Don't you see that's why they want to get there first?"

"Be quiet, man. You 're dreaming."

"Dreaming, was I? Anderson, Anderson, mate, I 'm not going mad. For God's sake, don't let me go mad."

"No, no, old man, it's all right. We 're on the right track now. Here, I 'll take the horse and you give me your arm. There, now then, if we 've luck we may hit Gerring Gerring before morning."

They walked on in silence, but Helm kept stumbling, and but for his companion's supporting arm would have fallen more than once. The moon rose up, and as it grew light as day again he stopped short and looked solemnly in his companion's face. It was worn and haggard and weary, but not so wild, he felt instinctively, as his own.

"Anderson," he said, "I know I 'm done for. My head's all wrong. It 's cooler now, but what'll it be to-morrow? If—if—if I do anything mad before I die, don't tell her, I 'd like her to think well of me. Just say I died, don't say how it hurt."

"All right, mate," said the other, for he had no comfort to give.

And then they walked on again in silence till the moon declined before the coming day, the cruel day, which brought the heat and the following crows again. Dawn brought them to a patch of "dead finish," as the settlers call a dense and thorny scrub with pretty green leaves, through which it is well nigh impossible to force a way even under the most favourable circumstances; and which presented an utterly impassable barrier to men in their condition. They turned aside once more, and Anderson thought to himself that they must indeed have given up hope, to be stopped by an impassable barrier and yet to make no moan. It was surely the very depths of hopelessness when all ways were alike to them. He looked back on their tracks and dismay filled his heart; they were not firm and straight, but wavering and wandering like those of men in the last extremity. He had followed tracks like these before now, and they always led to the same thing. He wondered dully would any one ever follow those tracks. A little further on Helm let go his arm and ran on ahead.

"We'll never do any good at this rate," he gasped, "never—never;" and he pulled at the collar of his shirt till he tore it away. "We must have something to drink. We 'll die else, and I mean to have a fight for life. There's the old horse, he can't stagger a step further; what's the good of keeping him? Let's shoot him—and—and—There's enough blood in him to—to—"

"No, no, man, no. I tell you that's the beginning of the end—more than the beginning—the end in fact."

"I don't care. I can't stand this;" and before Anderson could stop him, Helm had drawn his pistol and shot the horse in the head.

The poor beast was at his last gasp, and for the last hour Anderson had been meditating the advisibility of leaving him behind, so it was no material loss; his only care now was to prevent his mate from drinking the blood, which, according to the faith of the bushmen, is worse than drinking salt water.

"Poor old beggar," he said, taking his pistols and cartridges from the saddle, where they had been wrapped among the blankets, "I suppose it was about the kindest thing we could do for him. Come on, mate, we must leave him to the crows now," and he caught Helm's arm and would have led him on.

But the other resisted and breaking free ran back, and before he could stop him, had drawn his knife across the horse's throat and taken a long draught of blood.

Does it sound ghastly? But such things are, and his lips were dry and parched, and his throat so swollen that he could only speak in hoarse whispers, and so great was the temptation that Anderson, looking away at the bare pitiless plain, with the mocking mirage in the distance, felt that he too might as well drink and die; only the thought of the cripple boy who would be alone in the world but for him, made him make one more desperate effort for self-control.

He took the younger man's arm and dragged him on, skirting slowly round the "dead finish" till at length, late in the afternoon, it gave place to boree. His own senses were clear enough, but Helm was muttering wildly, and he listened with unheeding ears to his babble of home and mother and sweetheart. They could not go far, and soon they forced their way in among the scrub, and though the burning thirst was worse than ever, the shade was grateful. The crows stopped too, and settled on the low trees, turning their evil blue-black heads on one side to get a better view of their prey.

"I can't keep my head," moaned Helm, "I can't. I have been mad all day. I know I have. It has stretched out into ages this long day and it's not over yet. When were we lost? Yesterday? The day before? It feels like years."

"Never mind," said Anderson, not unkindly, "it can't be much longer now. Try to sleep, old man."

"Sleep! with a thousand devils tearing at me!"

But they did sleep after all, a wearied, troubled sleep, a broken sleep full of frightful dreams, or still more cruel ones of cooling streams and rippling waters. Night came, and Anderson awoke from what seemed to him a doze of a moment to find his companion gone from his side. For a second the thought came to him that it was not worth while to look for him. He was mad—mad, and where was the use of troubling about him any further; and then his better feelings, and perhaps that longing for human companionship which we all must feel, made him rise up and look for him. Up and down, he was staggering up and down, a hundred feet one way and then back again on his own tracks.

"We must get on, old chap," he muttered when he saw Anderson, "we must get on. You rest if you like though; there isn't anybody waiting for you; but Mabel, she 's waiting for me and I must try and get back. She would be disappointed else. Grieve! of course she'll grieve if I'm lost. All the world isn't a cynic like you."

Anderson took his arm again.

"We'll go together," he said. "If you do care a straw about seeing her again, come on quietly with me."

He yielded for the moment, but it required one continuous effort on Anderson's part to keep him up to it. Plainly his reason was gone, and the other man, growing weaker and weaker, found by the time the sun was high in the heavens that the effort was more than he could make. It was the end, or so close that he could only hope and pray the end would come quickly. The young fellow had struggled on so bravely, so hopefully, and now it had come to this. They had left the scrub behind them and Anderson made his way to a tree, the only specimen of its kind in all the wide plain, and lay down beneath its branches—to rest? No, he felt in his heart it was to die. Helm he could not persuade to lie down. He kept staggering on hopelessly round and round the tree, struggling to keep in the shade, fancying, as many a lost man has done before him, that he was "pushing on."

It was the same old story. Anderson had heard it told hundreds of times over the camp fire, one man will lie down to die quietly, and the other will go raving mad. So Helm had gone mad, poor chap; and then he remembered his passionate prayer to him, not to let him go mad, to shoot him if he saw he was going mad, and he lay and looked up at the hard blue sky through the leaves, and at the watching crows, and knew that he was only waiting for death, knew that he was too utterly weary to aid in any way his mate. He listened to him muttering to himself for a little, watched him as he went monotonously round and round. It was not so hard after all—not near so hard for him as for Helm. If only the boy were dead, he thought wearily, if only the boy were dead he would be glad that this should end it, his life was never worth much, he had failed all through, he would be glad to be at rest— if only the boy were there before him; but the boy—the poor little helpless thing, he must make another effort for the boy's sake, and he struggled to his feet again. But the burning landscape was a blood-red blur before his eyes, and then, quite suddenly it seemed to him, sight and hearing left him. He was dying—was this death? How merciful death was—if only the boy—

Very wearily he opened his eyes. Could it be that some one was pouring water down his throat? Some one was bathing his face.

"He's coming to," said a voice in his ear. "By Jove, it was a narrow shave. The other poor chap's done for, isn't he, Ned?"

"Quite dead. He went mad evidently, clean off his head. Why, the poor chap had begun on his own grave."

When Anderson came to himself he found he had been picked up by the other exploring party.

"We picked up your tracks away by the 'dead finish' there," said the leader, "and I thought it must be pretty near up with you. You 've had the devil's own luck, mate. Why, you were within five miles of Gerring Gerring Water, and over by the 'dead finish' you passed within three miles of a very decent waterhole, quite good enough to have kept life within you. You shot the horse?"

"My mate did. He was mad, poor fellow."

"Poor beggar, he seems to have had a bad time, but it's all over now."

It was indeed all over now. They had wrapped him in a blanket and were digging a shallow grave. He had begun it himself, they said, and had been digging with his long knife, though whether it was for water, or whether it was really intended for a grave, no one could now say. His sufferings were ended.

They left him there in the desert, the young fellow who had fought so hard for his life and set so much store by it, and as soon as Anderson was a little recovered, set out for Yerlo again.

It was over a week before he reached the station, so far had he wandered out of the track, and as he rode up to the house a stable boy lounged up to him.

"What a while you 've been away, Boss," he said. "We 'd most given you up for lost. The mail's in and there's a pile of letters for Mr. Helm. None for you though."

"Is everything all right?" asked Anderson, feeling like a man who had come back from the grave.

"N-o-o, there's mighty bad news. I don't like to tell though."

"Out with it, man, don't keep me waiting."

The lad looked away and turned his pipe from side of his mouth to the other.

"It 's your youngster," he said. "He had convulsions last Sunday. Mrs. Brook—she said as nothing couldn't have saved him. 'It was a blessed release,' she said."

Anderson flung the reins to the lad and walked quietly into the house. It was a mistake, he clearly saw, coming back from the grave. He wished he had died within five miles of Gerring Gerring Water.

THE LOSS OF THE "VANITY

"You don't care. Oh! Susy, you don't care!

"But I do," she sobbed. "You know, you know I care."

They were standing on a jutting headland, looking away out over the Southern Ocean, and the sea, blue and calm as the sky above, stretched out before them. Behind them were the low forest-clad ranges that bounded the coast line, shutting out the lonely selection from the rest of the colony of Victoria, and the only sign of human habitation was the weatherboard farmhouse the girl called home. Even that was hardly visible from where they stood, hidden as it was by the swell of the hill, and alone here with this man, alone with the sea and sky around her, with the soft South wind blowing among her curls, with the plaintive cry of the seagulls in her ears, the salt savour of the sea in her nostrils, she was sorely tempted to throw off the trammels of her education, to do the thing her heart prompted her to do, to tell this man he was dearer, as she felt in her heart he was dearer, than anything on earth. But so much stood in the way. For twenty years she had lived secluded in this lonely corner of the earth, all her thoughts, her hopes, her fears, bounded by the horizon of her own home, and the narrow limits of the township, just five miles away on the other side of the ranges. And now this sailor man, brought home by her young apprentice brother, had come into her life, bringing new thoughts, new ideas, new—she whispered it to herself, with a hot blush—hopes.

Five-and-twenty years ago now, Angus Mackie and his wife had emigrated from the cold and stormy western isles of Scotland to this sunny South land, and they had brought with them to their new home the stern faith of the old Puritan, the rigid adherence to the old rules, the hard, straitlaced life, and so had they brought up the children that grew up around their hearth. And Susy was the eldest, Susy with the blue eyes and rose-leaf complexion, and waving chestnut hair. So pretty she was, this daughter of the South, it hardly seemed possible she could be the child of the stern Puritan parents, and yet she had grown up in their ways, grave and obedient, walking in the narrow path set so straight before her without a question, and without a doubt. Never for one moment had she looked over the hedges with which she was set about— hardly had she realized there were hedges—and now this man had come like a fresh breeze from the sea, and he had taught her—what had he not taught her? At his glance all the passion born of the blue skies and the bright sunlight, and the warm breezes of her native land, awoke to life, and filled her heart with thoughts and longings that she, untutored, and ignorant of the world's ways, hardly understood. Only she leaned against the rock that cropped up out of the hillside, and pressed up against it till the hard stone marked her hands. Perhaps the physical pain brought her some rest from the mental disquietude which was so new to her.

The man who stood beside her was a sailor every inch of him. Not handsome perhaps, but certainly good-looking, with honest blue eyes, and a steadfast strong face. A man who had read and thought, and even though now at five-and-twenty he was but second mate of the *Vanity*, had lived his life to some purpose, for the fates had been against him; it had been an uphill struggle always, and in uphill struggles we have little time for the niceties of life. And now this girl, this dainty, fair, feminine thing had come across his path like a gleam of the sunshine of her own land, and when he felt he had fairly won her, his very honesty set a barrier in his way.

"You know I care," she sobbed. She would have used a stronger word, but shyness prevented her, and she put her face down on her clasped hands, and sobbed aloud.

"If you love me," he said deliberately; he was not shy now, though he turned away from her bowed head, and looked away over the sea sparkling in the November sunshine, "if you love me, what is there in God's name to stand between us?"

"That," she said, in a whisper, "just that."

"What?"

She lifted up her head now, and looked away at the sea too, but she did not see it, for her eyes were misty with tears. And he did not see that, for he too looked seaward. Far too deeply moved were they to look each other in the face.

"You know," she said; and in her voice the trace of the Scotch accent which still lingered there, inherited from her father, was softened by the Australian drawl, which, whatever other folks might think, sounded infinitely sweet in Harper's ears, "you know," she repeated again, "you know," and there was an appeal in the soft voice, a prayer that he would not force her too far.

But he had gone too far for pity. In plain words she had told him she loved him, and in plain words now would he have named the bar that she had set up between them.

"What is it?" he asked, and his voice sounded cold and hard, "in heaven's name, what is it!"

"You know," she hesitated, "it is written—that—that we shall have no—no dealings—with—with the unrighteous."

"Am I unrighteous?" he asked bitterly. "How am I unrighteous?"

"You are an unbeliever. You—you told me so yourself. You don't believe in heaven or—or—hell—or—or—"

"In heaven or hell, don't I? You know, Susy—good Lord!—Susy, you know you can make this world one or the other for me.

"Don't—don't," she implored. "I mean you don't think enough about your eternal salvation."

"Child, how can I? This world is hard enough to get on in, God knows, how can I worry about the next? Who knows? There mayn't be a next."

"There is, there is!" she cried, eagerly. "Oh! if you would only repent while there is yet time—if you would only repent and be saved!"

"Oh, child, child, is there anything in the world I would not do for your sweet face?"

"Not for me—oh, not for me! Because—because—"

He put up his hand to stop her. The religious phrases that she had been accustomed to from her youth up, and that came naturally to her tongue, hurt him somehow as the foul-mouthed conversation of the fo'c'sle had never hurt him. From her lips he would not, if he could help himself, hear the phrases he had been accustomed to laugh at as canting and hypocritical.

"Don't dear, don't. I know what you are going to say. It is no good. We are so different altogether. I can't believe—as you believe—I cannot. I 'll do my best to be a good man—I 'll never lie to you or—"

"It is no use," she moaned, "no use at all. We cannot prevail by our own strength."

He laughed bitterly.

"Belief is not a matter of will," he said, "or I would believe just to please you—just because I want you more than anything in the wide world. All I can do is to be honest, and tell you I can't believe. It need never make any difference to you, dear, never, never."

The girl laid her face down on the hard rock again.

"And if—and if—next time your ship goes past here you were to fall from the mast, and be drowned, you think—you think you would just go out like a fire—that—that would be all."

He kicked a stone till it fell over the edge of the cliff, and they could hear it going by leaps and bounds into the sea a hundred feet below.

"And you think," he said, "I shall be eternally damned, tormented in fire and brimstone for ever and ever. Upon my word, Susy, mine is the kinder fate."

"I can't bear to think of it, I can't bear to think of it!" she cried. "Oh! Ben, Ben! I can't bear it!"

He made a step forward then and caught her in his arms. How could he resist the upturned face and the sweet blue eyes brimming with tears. Puritan she might be, the old Covenanter blood might be strong as ever, but she loved him—there was little doubt of that, and he clasped her close in his arms and covered her face with kisses.

"What does it matter, dear, what does it matter? Let the future take care of itself."

She tried to wrench herself from his embrace then.

"No, no, it is for eternity. I can't, I can't."

"Susy," he caught both her hands in his, "do you love me?"

"You know I do."

"Better than any one in the world?"

"Yes." She whispered it under her breath, as if afraid of her own temerity.

"Then listen. You shall do as you like with me. I 'll give up the sea, darling. I 'll take up a selection here, you shall teach me your creed and I 'll do my best to believe. There, my little girl, will that satisfy you? Who knows, in time I may become as respectable a psalm-singer as that holy swab, Clement Scott, your father's so fond of quoting. The beggar's got a tenderness for you, hasn't he, Susy? Why the first week I was here I was wild with jealousy of the canting brute!"

Gently but firmly she drew herself out of his encircling arms and leaned up drearily against the rock again.

"Clement Scott," she said, and there was a hopeless ring in her voice that went to his heart like a knife, "Clement Scott is a true Christian man, he is father's friend, and—and—oh!—" with a sudden burst of passion, "I know—I know he is the better man."

Ben Harper said nothing, only moved a step or two further seaward. What could he say? The girl loved him, he saw that she loved him well and truly, but she did not love him well enough. She wanted to put him aside, as her training taught her she ought to put aside all the pleasures of this life, all the sunshine and laughter of life, as things hurtful to her soul's salvation. And because she was young, because she had been born under sunny, laughter-loving skies, his love came to her with a cruel temptation, and because of its very strength, because of the pain it cost her, she would put it aside as a thing wrongful and wicked.

He looked at the silent little figure in its pink gingham frock, leaning up against the rock with head bowed down on its clasped hands. Dimly he understood the struggle that was going on in her breast, and clearly too he foresaw the inevitable end. Her very love for him was an argument against him. Never, never, never!—the booming sea on the rocks below seemed to take up the refrain—would this woman be wife of his? Never, never, never; the play was played out. Down through the vista of years he looked, and saw her the wife of the man he hated—the man who was to him the very incarnation of hypocrisy and cant He saw the hard, loveless life; he saw the lines growing in the fair, young face that was so dear to him; he saw stern Duty take the place of Love; he saw her life grow hard and narrow; he read in her face the bitterness of unfulfilled hopes, and the longing, the unutterable longing for something that might not be put into words, and a great pity for her filled his heart. Not for worlds would he add to her pain. She had come into his life, a dainty, fair, tender thing, and he had only hurt her; by his own pain he gauged hers.

A step forward and he was looking down at the snow-white breakers thundering at the foot of the cliff. The sea was his home, the cruel, fickle sea; he would go back to it and leave the woman he loved in peace. What right had he to come into her life to spoil it? He would go back whence he came, and all should be as it had been before. Go back?—ah! we none of us can go back; surely the Greeks of old were right when they said that not even Omnipotence itself can alter the past. For him he felt, as he watched the white gulls wheel about the face of the inaccessible cliff, there could be no comfort. He had gotten a hurt that would last him a lifetime, but for her— surely he had not hurt her irredeemably.

Very slowly he walked back to her side again, and laid a hand on her shoulder.

"Susy," he said, and he strove with all his strength to banish from his voice all else but kindness, "are you—do you—are you going to marry Clement Scott?"

But she would not raise her face.

"My father—he—I mean—" and so low was her voice, he had to stoop his head to hear, "father said I should—he is a Godfearing man—my father said I—I should beware that I chose—the—the better man. It—it—would be for my soul's salvation."

"Susy—Susy, child, I would not harm you, not for all this world or the next could give me. See now, my darling, I must go and leave you, must I?"

She raised her face now, and the bright sunlight showed it to him white and strained. She was paying for her love, if ever woman was. It went to his heart to see her quivering lips, to read in her eyes that voiceless appeal to him, not to tempt her beyond her strength.

"My poor little girl!"

He put out his arms and drew her close to his breast again, and at the sound of his voice, at the tender touch of his hands, she broke down—broke down and cried passionately with her face hidden on his shoulder. He pushed back her hat, and some strands of her hair fell loose across his hand. He held it lightly and tenderly, noting how it shone in the sunlight, noting that it looked like spun gold.

"Don't cry like that, my darling, it breaks my heart to hear you."

But he knew there was no hope for him in those tears. There was resignation, heartbroken resignation to the inevitable, but not a touch of yielding, not a spark of hope for him.

"My poor little girl!" he said again. "My poor little girl!"

"It is my poor boy, I think," she sobbed, "if you care, my poor, poor Ben!"

She was so close and yet so far, so very far away from him.

"Susy, child, I can't bear this," his voice was hoarse with the passion that now he could not keep under control, "you must let me go—now."

She raised her face and looked with her tear-dimmed eyes straight into his.

"Ben, Ben, I love you, I *will* tell you this once, whether it's right or wrong. I love you, I love you, I love you!" And she flung her arms round his neck, and drawing down his face to her own covered it with kisses, hot, passionate kisses in which the future, which for her stretched away into eternity, was forgotten.

"I must go. Susy, Susy, if you will not have me, in pity's name let me go!"

"Go then, go, my darling."

She drew herself out of his arms firmly, sadly, and they stood for a moment looking into each other's eyes, only for a moment though, then with a long-drawn sigh she turned away and covered her face with her hands.

He stood a little apart and took a long farewell to all his hopes. Would the picture ever fade from his mind, he wondered. There it all lay before him, blue sea and sky and dark bushland, and the only living thing visible the trembling girl in her simple pink frock, her face hidden in her hands, and the sunlight bringing out lines of gold in her fair hair. So it ended—his month-old romance. To-day he must go back to the old dull routine that makes up the sum of a sailor's life, and this brief madness must be but a tender memory of the past.

"Susy," he whispered, "Susy," but the little figure never raised its head.

"Susy, won't you wish me good-bye. Say something to me before I go. Must I go?"

He had no hope she would change her mind. He had learned her steadfastness only too well in the last four weeks, only he asked because it gave him the faintest shadow of an excuse for stopping at her side.

"Yes, go, go!" And the command was almost prayerful in its intensity.

"But—but—one word—one word—you—"

"God bless you! God keep you! Go, go!"

He turned away then, away from the bright water sparkling in the sunlight, away from the woman he loved with all his strength; but a chimera, it seemed to him, a vague fancy, stood between them, yet it was stronger than iron bars, and with a heavy sigh he turned his face towards the dark ranges and went down to the township, five miles beyond.

The good ship *Vanity* had lain three long months at Port Melbourne Pier, but they were weighing anchor at last. Standing there on the poop, the second mate listened sadly enough to the chanting of the men as they walked slowly round the capstan. There was almost a wail in the tune, though the words were the essence of common-placeness, and related how the singers had courted Sally Brown for seven years, and when she had proved obdurate, with great complacency had taken her daughter instead.

"Seven long years I courted Sally,

Ay, ay, roll and go!

Seven long years and she wouldn't marry,

Spend my money on Sally Brown."

"Ay! ay!" it rose loud and clear above the noise of the busy pier, above the voices of the men at work there, above the creaking and groaning of the crane that was loading the great iron tank that lay next them, "ay! ay! roll and go!"

Yes, he was going now, leaving all the sunshine of his life behind him, the best part of his life and—

"Now then, mister, bear a hand there, ain't there longshore lubbers enough wi'out you?"

"Ay! ay! roll and go!" It was only another way of saying "Blessed be drudgery," only a reminder that work is a universal panacea for all ills and heartaches. And after all the second mate of the sailing-ship is not likely to have much time for idle dreams—regretful or otherwise—for the life of such men is monotonous enough; and two days later when they had come through the Rip, and were out in the Southern Ocean sailing along eastward, there was little enough to remind Ben Harper of the events of a week before. True it was on this stern, forbidding coast lay the Mackie selection; it was over this expanse of sea they two had stood and looked when they said farewell—he had even heard tell that the lights from their cottage window, the bright glow from the kitchen fire, were plainly visible to ships at sea, so close was she. And he wondered to himself should he see those lights to-night. Hardly. He lay there in his bunk and listened to the row in the rigging. Things had not mended evidently since he went below. Gone was the summer and the bright November sunshine, the wind from the south was coming up cold and chill, and the prospect of four hours to-night on a very cold, wet, bleak poop was anything but inviting.

"It 's just going eight bells, sir." He scrambled out of his bunk and into some clothes and oilskins, and was standing alongside the mate under the lee of the weather cloth in the rigging, by the time the watch got aft. They were the average crew of a sailing ship, men from every nation under the sun, and as they passed slowly round the capstan, their shoulders hunched to their ears, each man answered sullenly to his name. Not that they bore the second mate any ill-will, but Jack ashore spends his last weeks in riotous living and suffers a slow recovery for the first few days of the voyage. Besides the night was bitter cold, the wind that whistled shrilly through the rigging already bore on its chill breath drops of icy rain; there was no prospect of things mending, and after the hot summer days at Port Melbourne extra wraps—indeed any clothes in the fo'c'sle beyond what each man stood up in—were conspicuous by their absence. Merchant Jack is a thriftless beggar at best, and who could have foreseen wintry weather like this?

"Andersen!" called the mate, as a tall, fair haired Swede, his hairy breast bare to the cold night air, stepped forward.

"Sir."

"Muntz!"

"Herr."

"Reed!"

"'Ere, sir."

"Portross!"

"Sah-h."

What a motley crew they were! Swedes and Germans, cockneys and niggers, they passed on till the two watches had answered to their names, and the last man was a Russian Finn, black-haired and swarthy, with a flat face and eyes like a Tartar.

"They Finns," said the bo'sun confidentially to Harper, "is just pisen. Never knew no ship come to any good as carried em.

"Pooh!" said the second mate, who was not troubled with superstitious fears; besides the bo'sun made the same remark every time the watches were mustered, then he shouted, "Relieve the wheel and look out. Keep yourselves handy there, the watch."

"She 's got the main-to'g'll'nts'le on, mister," said the mate, "and the outer jib. It's been like this all the watch, steady enough. The sea's getting up a bit, and having the spanker set makes her steer so badly, but the old man wouldn't let me douse it;" and muttering something about the "glass going right down into the hold" the oil-skinned figure departed down the companion.

It was dark, very dark indeed, for though the moon was nearly full, heavy clouds obscured the sky, and only now and then she managed to pierce them, showing as clear as day the deserted wet decks—for the watch had all stowed away—the few sails set and just under the foot of the foresail the lookout man, banging his arms to and fro to keep himself warm.

The second mate paced briskly up and down the poop, for'ard was the lookout man, aft the man at the wheel, they three seemed to compose the whole ship's company, and it gave him for a moment a sense of loneliness. Hardly a week ago and he had hoped for such different things.

He had lost nothing, nothing; he told himself so over and over again, as he drew his oilskins close round him, and yet there was a sense of loss in his life, a great and terrible loss. She would be nothing to him, the girl he loved so well, she would marry Clement Scott, she had as good as told him so—because—because he was the better man. The better man—the better man—the words formed themselves into a sort of rhythm that his steps kept time to—"the better man, the better man."

"Binnacle light's goin' hout, sir," said the man at the wheel, breaking in on his sad thoughts.

"Below there. One of you boys trim this light."

Young Angus Mackie answered his hail, unshipped the light, and lingered for a moment.

"We 'll be right aboard t'auld place in an hour or two, sir."

"What?"

"I was sayin' that goin' on this tack we 'll be awfu' close in shore. Ye could pretty nigh chuck a biscuit in at the kitchen door. I wonder if they'll be thinkin' o' us."

"E—h—h?" muttered Harper, for had not his thoughts been taking the same road, though not for worlds would he have owned it.

"I'm thinkin' Susy will. Ye see I 'm thinkin' Susy was a bit gone—"

"You boy, trim that lamp," said Harper angrily. "Look here, my lad, you just keep your tongue lashed amidships, and don't go gassing about things that don't concern you in the least, or you and I 'll part brass rags."

The boy scurried below and returned with the lamp retrimmed. He slipped the light into the binnacle and looked doubtfully at the second mate. It was dull and he was inclined to talk, but after his late rebuff hardly dared. Harper began to pace up and down again, and the boy stowed himself under the lee of the house, volunteering the information as he passed the mate.

"Bo'sun says the wind 's goin' to shift ahead."

"You be hanged, and the bo'sun too!"

But before an hour had gone by he was obliged to acknowledge that the bo'sun's weather prophecies were very correct, for the wind shifted point after point till it was right ahead and blowing half a gale. Harper looked aloft and noted the clouds scurrying across the sky. Heavier and heavier they were growing to wind'ard.

"By Jove!" he muttered to himself, "we 're in for a nasty night."

Suddenly the lookout man reported, "Light right ahead, sir."

Harper stepped forward to the skylight and peered down into the cabin, dimly lighted by an oil lamp. It was a bare enough little place at best, but it looked comfort itself as contrasted with the wet decks above. The skipper was lying on a settee sound asleep, one hairy arm thrown out, and on the table meditatively surveying him was Dinah, the ship's cat.

"Hallo there!" reported the mate through the skylight; "light right ahead, sir."

Very lazily he rolled off the sofa, scared puss out of her senses by a rough sweep of his hand, and came up on deck.

"Great Scott!" he growled, "what a night!" Then he took a squint through his night glasses.

"Oh, yes, mister," he said, "that's all right. It's just a small light—a leading mark for the small craft going into the creek there for lime. Fixed white light, I heard of it the day before we left. It's deep water right up. We'll go right in, mister, and make a long board of it on the next tack."

The moon was completely hidden now, and both men hanging over the break of the the poop could see nothing but the bright light right ahead.

"It looks small, sir," ventured Harper, taking another look through his glasses.

"Didn't I tell ye it was small? If ye will be for ever—"

Harper still looked steadily through his glasses.

"By the Lord! sir, that looks uncommonly like a line of breakers! There—to port!"

The skipper made one hesitating step forward, and then the truth flashed on him like lightning.

"Great Scott!" he cried again, "so it is! Call all hands. Hands 'bout ship!" Then he turned to the man at the wheel, who was the Russian Finn the bo'sun objected to as unlucky, "Keep her clean full for stays."

The men came tumbling out from the holes and corners where they had stowed away, and the watch below came up growling audibly at having their rest disturbed, but none apparently understanding the danger of the situation. It is all in the day's work that a sailor should be disturbed before he has had more than a taste of the bliss of sleep. The wild tumbling waters and the shrieking wind told them no tale; they only thought the wind had gone round and freshened a bit since they went below.

Harper standing on the fife rail at the crojack braces could have told them a different story. Clearly he saw the danger. There ahead, a little to leeward, were the long line of breakers; even in this pitchy darkness he could see their white foam-topped crests against the inky water; he fancied that even above the roaring of the wind through the rigging he could distinguish the crash with which they flung themselves hungrily against the rocks, the long-drawn sob as of disappointment with which they fell back into the sea again, there to gather strength for a fresh onslaught. Above them was the loom of the land showing only like thick cloud-bank against the horizon, and the bright light beckoning, it seemed, with friendly hands.

"Ready about!" shouted the skipper.

"O—o—oh, o—o—oh, o—o—oh!" sang the men at the braces in mournful monotone. Bang went the wet sail against the mast, and the second mate from his vantage point watched her slowly come up to wind. Slowly—

slowly—the towering seas came pouring aboard—she took it in by the deck-house by ton loads, and the men all hung on to the nearest thing handy for dear life. Slowly, slowly her nose came up to the wind. Would she go round? Would she? Would she?

"Gummy!" he heard the bo'sun's voice near him in the darkness, and above all the din; "she is a blanked old bathing machine, ain't she?"

Nobody disputed the fact. Would she come round? Would she? Would she? Surely she was coming.

Then there was a pause for a brief second. Every man in that pause, it seemed, realized the gravity of the situation.

By Jingo! Will she come? Will she not?

Then the hoarse voice of the skipper broke in.

"Up with your helm, hard up! Flatten in your head sheets! Haul in your weather cro'jack brace!"

"Jammed, by G—d!" said the bo'sun, taking a squint over the side at the racing water and the ship rolling helplessly in the trough of the seas, "jammed, by G—d! like Jackson's cat."

The ship was in irons. "Would they ever get out of this fix?" thought Harper, while he listened to the skipper shouting orders to the man at the wheel, as she gathered stern-way and heard the Russian Finn's hoarse:

"Helm's amidships, sir," in reply. He was a plucky old man, old Alick MacDonald, given to carrying on as long as he dared, which was a good deal longer than most men would have dared, and his second mate had seen him in some very tight places already, but his good luck had always stood him in good stead; would it hold good once more?

Gradually the ship paid off, slowly her nose came round, and Harper, looking at the foaming line of breakers, thought how perilously close they were. But—but—surely after all she would come through scot free, a moment more—only a moment more. The moon came from behind the heavy clouds paling the light ashore before her bright rays, and showing them just for a second the seething white water all around. So close was the danger, every man held his breath.

"We're clear!" The words were on Harper's lips, then—crash—the ship struck with a sickening shock that shook her from stem to stern, and brought down the foreto'g'll't mast from aloft with all its tackle, and strewed the deck with wreckage. In a moment the men had dropped the ropes and rushed as one man aft to be clear of the falling top hamper.

"Stand fast, men, stand fast!" sung out Harper. "Where are you off to there?"

"Well," growled the bo'sun, who still stood by the second mate, "hell's the next port, if you ask me!" And his companion could not but wonder at his coolness. He too, clinging for life, realized that the good ship *Vanity* was a total wreck, and as he realized it, he raised his eyes and saw the light, which had been their guiding star till now, go suddenly out and leave all the cliff in pitchy darkness.

Crash went the ship again, bumping heavily and bringing down more hamper from aloft to add to the confusion on deck, and sea after sea swept over her. The two men scrambled aft, and above the thunder of the seas that fell aboard and the roar of the breakers that were not to be disappointed of their prey, heard the skipper shouting orders for the launching of the life-boat. It seemed to Harper no boat could live in such a raging sea, of a surety no boat could land on such a coast—at least not the coast as he knew it, the coast where was the Mackie selection—and the Mackie selection was somewhere hereabouts, you might see the light of their kitchen fire from—Good God! it came upon him like a flash—was that the light that had led them to destruction?

But there was no time for questions like that. The idea passed through his mind as he heard the skipper shout,

"Port watch, rig tackles! Starboard watch, see port life-boat all clear for going out!"

The raging wind and sea seemed to have gone down for a moment, now they had accomplished their end. The moon came out again, and he saw the watch at the skids, and the tall figure of the first mate as he stood on the boat, ripping off the covering with a sheath knife. One step forward he made to go to his assistance when there rose a towering wall of dark water to wind'ard.

"Stand from under—stand from under!" yelled every throat, but it was too late. It was doubtful if they heard, it was certain they had no time to get away. The wave came on resistlessly, and when the water had passed over them, boat and skids, part of the bulwarks, the first mate, and half the starboard watch had been swept away. There was a wailing cry above the roar of the seas, but it was impossible to say who had gone.

"Gone to port," muttered the bo'sun, "an' darned quick too!" And that was their requiem, for now it was each man for himself. The old skipper's voice was silent, and the second mate feared he too must have been carried overboard by the last sea.

"Jump for a blue light," he said to a boy next him, who was clinging to the broken skylight, "they're in the locker in the cabin."

The lad hesitated, then swung himself down, and in a minute or so returned, clambering back through the skylight holding two blue lights in his hand. He struck the end of one and illuminated the whole place with the ghastly glare. The *Vanity*, but a few minutes before a trim, smart ship, lay there on the reef a total wreck. The bright light showed her broken bulwarks with the seas making clean sweeps through them, the decks one mass of wreckage in hopeless confusion, cordage and rigging, splintered yards, and shattered deck-house—all alike had suffered a sea change. The foremast and the mainmast were gone, and their stumps stood up jagged and torn, but the mizzen lower mast still remained, and the men—those of them that were left—were in the rigging, for the deck every moment was becoming more untenable. The wheel was broken and the Russian Finn lay dead beside it, killed by a falling gaff, his swarthy face, white now in the bright light, turned up to the stormy sky; and a little farther for'ard, close to where Harper himself was standing, lay the skipper, jammed against the skylight by a heavy hencoop.

He bent over him and attempted to move the hencoop.

"All right, mister," said the old man bitterly, "better leave it alone. The old barkie's clean done for, an' I'm thinkin' we 're all bound for the same port."

As the blue light died down the lad lighted another, and one or two men dropped from the rigging and crawled to Harper's assistance.

"I ain't worth much now, mister," moaned the old man again; uwe 'll never get out of this fix; "but they succeeded in dragging him aft and lashing him in the rigging. The boy who had burned the blue lights scrambled after them, and then, clinging there, hardly out of reach of the hungry waves, commenced their long wait for daylight.

"What 's the time, sir?" asked the lad next the second mate.

"About eleven."

The boy drew a long sigh.

"Oh, Lordy! we can never hold on till morning, can we?"

"God knows."

A light started out of the darkness against the cliff—a light that grew and grew till it was a great flame even from where they stood, and the men in the rigging raised a shout.

"They see us ashore! Hurrah! hurrah!"

"Mighty little good their seeing us ashore 'll do us," said the bo'sun; "hell 's between!" And looking at the strip of seething boiling water that lay between them and the coast, Harper was obliged to acknowledge the man was right.

Still it lent them some comfort—that bright fire. They were a handful of men clinging there, drenched to the skin already, and every wave wetted them again with its salt spray, the wind whistled through the rigging bitter and cold, the icy rain like spear points cut their faces; there was no hope for them, no hope at all save in that blazing fire on shore.

Who shall describe the thoughts of men in extremity? Who shall say whether they thought at all—those men half dead with cold, clinging for dear life with numb hands to a slender rope that might give way at any moment? Would they see the morning light?

Harper was surprised to find he took it so quietly. There was none of the despair he had fancied he should feel in like case—or rather, he questioned, was it not despair that made him take it so calmly, utter despair? And after all what did a few years more or less of life matter to him? If death only came quickly without much pain, would it not be well with him? What had he to live for? Bitterly came back to him the last time he had looked over this raging sea. If it was not here, it was somewhere hereabouts, somewhere quite close. He could not help thinking of it, and contrasting it, that lovely summer's afternoon, and this bitter winter's night, with just ten days in between them. He looked at the fire on shore, now dying down, now blazing up brightly, replenished by willing hands, and between it and him came Susy Mackie's fair face. So sweet and dainty and fair, all that a man might long for, and yet she would give no thought to him. No thought! A wave higher than its fellows drenched him through and through, and made him wonder was the Vanity settling down, slipping off the reef into the deep water beyond it. No thought! What did it matter? It was only a little nearer the inevitable end, and if she had given him thought—if she had given him her heart, it was in despite her better judgment; her narrow up-bringing had won the day, and only that morning he had thought that life was not worth living without her. Why should he repine now that fate had taken him at his word? Then a great wave of tenderness came over him. His little girl, his sweet, pretty little girl, who made even of the stern, hard, unlovable faith of her fathers, a thing that was holy and beautiful. His little girl! He remembered—and the very thought sent a warm glow through his chilled veins—how she had wept over his possible death, wept bitter tears because she thought her God was harder and more cruel than the children He had made with His hands. His little girl, his darling!

The boy next him began to moan, and in spite of the shrieking wind and the howling sea Harper made out that his hands were aching, that he was perished with cold and could not hold on any longer.

"Nonsense, lad, nonsense!" and he took off his strong leather belt and buckled it round the shroud and round the boy's body, "there, that 'll give you a helping hand. Hold on now." Then as the boy thanked him, he saw by a stray and watery moonbeam it was young Angus Mackie.

"It's right on your own coast, Angus, we 've come to grief."

"I 'm thinking," said the lad, "it's right on our own place. I 'm thinkin' yon light—not the fire, the one we saw first—is our ain kitchen fire. Mony 's the time I 've been seein' it an' me out fishin' here."

"But the fireplace doesn't face the door," wondering to himself why it was he discussed such things now.

"Naw, but there 's a bit mirror agin the wall, it reflects things. Oh, mony's the time I've seen it. Mither, she wanted it in the parlour; but Susy, she was saying we were living in the kitchen, and it made things brighter like. Dad, he was for sayin' it was a snare o' the Evil One; but Susy, she had her way."

So after all it was his sweetheart's natural girlish longing after pretty bright things that had lured them to destruction. Should he die to-night it was her innocent hand that had dealt the blow. The boy beside him was thinking the same thing, and presently he said, "When she comes to know, what'll she say?"

Harper said nothing. If it had been possible he would have prayed the boy to keep the knowledge from her; but he knew it was not possible. If any man escaped from this wreck, he would surely tell of the light they had mistaken for the new leading mark, and if they all perished—well—then there would be no need to plead for silence. The sea keeps her own secrets.

"Susy is gone on ye, sir," said the boy again, "why wouldn't ye have her?"

It hardly seemed strange to him now, the question he would have resented fiercely at any other time.

"Have her!" he repeated, and looking down, he noted that the last wave had left behind it a great crack in the deck, and he heard the skipper moaning, "Oh, the poor barkie, the poor barkie!" and knew that he too had seen it. "Have her? She wouldn't have me."

"But—but—she—"

"She didn't think I was good enough," explained Harper hastily.

"She told ye that!—oh, Lord! They 've been at her about that pious psalm-singer Clement Scott. Ye try again when we get ashore. She's goin' to stop a bit wi' Aunt Barnes, at South Yarra, this Christmas. T' auld girl hates t' psalm-singer, an' she 'll do the job for ye. Oh, Lord! oh, Lord! I 'm starved wi' the cold."

"It 's not so long now," said Harper, and suddenly he felt as if the night were stretching itself into interminable years. The bar that Susy had thought so hopeless, so insurmountable, was it really but a thing of straw? Was there really a chance for him yet? Was there really anything in the lad's careless words? And hope awoke again in his breast, and with the hope a raging bitterness against the fate that was putting a barrier once more between him and the attainment of those hopes. She loved him, she had acknowledged that she loved him, and now to be free to win her! The eagerness for life awoke in him again. Who said the world was dreary? Who said life was not worth living? A bright, fair world stretched enticingly before him, and he was dying. Yes, dying—they were all dying, the old ship was breaking up fast, and if succour did not come quickly—He drew a long breath and looked down through the rain, that was falling in torrents now, at the decks below. One moment all was hidden by the raging seas, the next by the faint moonlight he saw the cracks widening—widening—then came another great sea, and he felt the ship bump heavily on the rocks. No, it was the poorest chance that she should last till morning, they—these men hanging to the rigging—had no chance whatever of living in the sea that boiled around them. Wider and wider grew the cracks on deck, the water was pouring into the hold, and the cargo was being washed out of her. One bale of wool—two—three—rose up on the next wave. A bale of wool! What is a bale against a man's life? And yet the skipper was moaning pitifully over their loss.

"My great Scott! eighteen hundred bales of wool gone! What will the owners say? The poor old barkie! The poor old barkie! How shall I face the owners?"

So! so! and his chances of facing those owners seemed so pitifully small, and yet the old man's thoughts were full of it. Sometimes he moaned over the wife and children in faraway England, but not as one who gives up all hopes of seeing them again, only as one who maybe had brought them to bitter poverty and pain by his mischance, for would the owners give him another ship, now he had lost the old *Vanity?* "Hardly likely," he muttered to himself. "Hardly likely." And so the bitter night wore on. There was nothing to mark the hours as they passed. Now a man moaned a little, now another cried aloud that he could hold on no longer, that he must fall and die before morning. Always there was the sea, sweeping over the decks and halfway up the mast towards them, with wearisome monotony. Great squalls of rain came up every now and then, blotting out all else and making all round inky-black; then they passed, and the pale and watery moon showed them the shore quite close, and the raging waters between. The tongue of the ship's bell had broken loose somehow, and the wash of the sea made it toll with mournful cadence. It rose clear and loud, even above the shrieking of the gale, and Harper fitted its notes to his own words. "Never more," it seemed to say; and then, as a heavier sea than usual swept over the wreck, shaking her down to her very keel, "Never, never more."

And yet on shore the fire leaped and danced. Kindly anxious hands were feeding it, and it was impossible not to think that the men who would stay out on such a bitter night, were not doing all they knew for the help and succour of these helpless men. There were rocket apparatus stationed along the coast, and if the ship would only hold together long enough, why should they not all be saved? If she only would. Ben Harper was feverish in his desire for life now. He must live; he must see Susy once again, he must—he must! And eagerly he watched for the dawn.

So long the night, so long, so long. Is it a truth that our hours of gladness and our hours of pain are all of a length? Surely not. The night wore on, and it seemed to those waiting men that the longed-for morning would never come. But gradually the moon sank behind the dark mass of the land to leeward, and in the east came the first faint streaks of dawn.

A shout rose up from the weary waiting men, a shout Harper fancied he heard echoed faintly from the shore. Then the day was born, stormy and cold, and the light only showed them a handful of men clinging to a wreck, which each sea threatened to break into a thousand pieces.

"Merciful God!" cried the skipper, as the daylight showed him the full extent of his peril, "my poor wee wife!"

But if the daylight showed them their danger it showed them too that those on shore had not been unmindful of them. The ugly cliffs, steep and inaccessible, were not very high, and on the nearest point to the wreck, not indeed one hundred yards away, a little knot of men were getting ready the rocket apparatus. There were women there too, with shawls thrown over their heads, and Harpers heart beat as he thought of seeing his love again. Surely now—now that he came to her from the very jaws of death—cast up out of the cruel sea—she would not reject him. Would she not rather take it as a sign from her God that she was to wed this man? Surely she would. In another few minutes he would be by her side—a little longer and he might hold her in his arms again. How long—how long? O God! if they would only make haste. Could they not see that every moment was precious, that the old ship was breaking up fast?

He began to count the men in the rigging, nineteen of them, men and boys, and the skipper was helpless with a broken leg. It would take them some time to get off. And yet not so long though—once they had the rope aboard.

They got the apparatus fixed at last, and then "swish." They could not see anything, for it was broad daylight now, but they heard the sigh of the rocket as it passed and knew it had missed. A despairing cry went up from the perishing men, for they, like the second mate, were counting their chances and reckoning them poor indeed. It almost seemed a matter of minutes now.

Again the men on shore tried, and this time the shout that went up was one of triumph. The thin line lodged beautifully over the mast, and the men in their awkward position hauled it in, and it seemed as if they had home and happiness within their grasp when the block came along.

Very carefully they made the thick rope fast round the mizzen lower masthead, the bo'sun still brisk and cheerful after the terrible night which he had spent in the rigging, his only covering a pair of torn dungaree trousers.

"None of your darned men-o'-war slippery hitches about this," said he; and Harper, as he saw the breeches-buoy come along the stout cable, could have shouted as the men were doing. Here was happiness and safety—here was the woman he loved—nay, should he not say rather the woman who loved him—waiting on shore for him, and would she deny him now he had come through so much? His little girl, his darling! One by one he watched the men go, he watched the breeches-buoy swallowed up in the raging waters, he watched them received on shore as men risen from the dead, and he counted eagerly the moments till his turn should come. They knew now on shore the name of the ship. Was that woman on shore looking seaward, his Susy? She had a red shawl, he remembered, as we do remember trifles in the supreme moments of our life. That must be Susy, and she was thinking of him. Only six now. And now only five. For one brief moment he felt as if he were tasting the bliss of perfect happiness. Could he have doubted that a merciful God ruled this world of ours? Ah, little girl, you shall learn a newer, purer, more pitiful faith, and Ben Harper will be your teacher, and then—and then—— All the exultation went out of his heart, for his eye fell on the tail of the block and he saw that it was stranded. It had lain there—that thick rope—in its house, carefully kept against the day of need, day after day, week after week, year after year, and the long waiting had told on the stout rope, slowly it had rotted, slowly—and no man knew it. And now in the day of need when a good man's life depended on it, it was failing. Was it though? Only three more men. And now only two—only the old skipper and himself. No one had noticed the rope, and where was the good of speaking of it. He watched the breeches-buoy, coming back to them, and clearly, clearly he read as in letters of fire that one of those two must die. Twelve hours ago he would have given his life for the skipper's, gladly, willingly; but now—now it was different. It was his right to live, he' told himself fiercely—his right, just as it was the right of the skipper to be the last to leave the ship. He was an old man, what was his life to him?—loyal enough to his owners—a rough old sea-dog, hard and even cruel at times—he was old, he had lived his life, he must be the one to stay. Even for the wife and children's sake—the owners were not hard men—they would see they did not starve. And he must see Susy again—just hold her in his arms once again. Sweetheart, sweetheart, who so dear in all the world? It was his right to go, he told himself again. Then he cut the lashings with which they had bound the skipper to the mast, the breeches-buoy was so close now and it was easier for him to do it. The old man might find a difficulty by himself, and he would want to be all clear when next the buoy came back. When next the buoy came back! He looked at the stranded rope and knew that the buoy would never come back. Hardly would it reach the shore. Certain it was it would never come back, and the wreck was breaking up fast. It was his right to go, and no one would know. And even if they did, he was only taking his rights. How could he give his life, with all its fair possibilities, all its high hopes, for this worn-out old shellback? And the buoy was here!

"You go, sir. It'll only make a few minutes' difference, and I can help you. You're hurt, and you'll find it hard to manage by yourself."

The old man demurred a moment—staunch old sailor, he would have stuck to the ship to the last, but the mate said again, "It only makes the difference of a minute or two, sir. That's nothing."

He could not send a message—not one. Why should he? They would never understand. The fair-haired girl would never know how he had longed for her this night.

Down, down went the buoy, and the waters swallowed it up. A great wave—another—he had done with life, for the rotten rope had parted at last!

But on shore there was great rejoicing, for they hauled the skipper up out of the sea, bruised and hurt and half drowned, but still alive; and the cry went round that he was the last man left aboard the Vanity.

Then the bo'sun put up his hands and squinted through them seaward.

"Jimini! there's the mizzen mast gone! Poor old girl!"

"An'," said another voice, the voice of the man who had left before the skipper, "there was two men aboard when I left, an' one of 'em was the second mate. Where is he?"

"Gone to ——," but a woman's bitter cry cut short the bo'sun's speech.

DICK STANESBY'S HUTKEEPER

"Hallo! Dick. You here! Why, I thought you were away up tea-planting in Assam."

"And I thought you were comfortably settled down on the ancestral acres by this time."

"No such luck. The ancient cousin is still very much to the fore. Has taken to himself a new wife in fact, and a new lease of life along with her. She has presented her doting husband with a very fine heir; and, well, of course, after that little Willie was nowhere, and departed for pastures new."

"Make your fortune, eh! Made it?"

"Of course. Money-making game riding tracks on Jinfalla! Made yours?"

"Money-making game riding tracks on Nilpe Nilpe."

The two men looked at each other, and laughed. In truth, neither looked particularly representative of the rank and aristocracy of their native land. The back blocks are very effectual levellers, and each saw in the other a very ordinary bushman, riding a horse so poor, the wonder was he was deemed worth mounting at all. Both were dusty and dirty, for the drought held the land in iron grip, and the fierce north wind, driving the dust in little whirls and columns before it, blew over plains bare of grass and other vegetation as a beaten road.

Around them was the plain, hot and bare of any living creature, nothing in sight save a low ridge bounding the eastern horizon, a ridge which on closer inspection took the form of bluffs, in most places almost inaccessible. Overhead was the deep blue sky, so blue it was almost purple in its intensity, with not a cloud to break the monotony. Sky and desert, that was all, and these two Englishmen meeting, and the shadows cast by themselves and their horses, were the only spots of shade for miles.

"Sweet place!" said Guy Turner, looking round. "Warmish too. Wonder what it is in the shade?"

"In the shade, man. There ain't any shade, unless you count the shadows of our poor old mokes, and mine's so poor, I 'll bet the sun can find his way through his ribs. I 've been in the sun since daybreak, and I reckon it is somewhere about boiling point."

"I suppose it must be over 1600. What the dickens did you come out for?"

"Well, seeing it's been like this for the last three months, and is likely to go on for three more, as far as I can see; it ain't much good stopping in for the weather; besides there's this valuable estate to be looked after. But to-day I rode over for the mails."

"What, to the head-station?"

"Lord, no! The track to Roebourne passes along about twenty miles off over there, and I get the boss to leave my mail in a hollow tree as he passes."

"Trusting, certainly. There 's some good about this God-forsaken country."

Dick Stanesby, or, to give him his full name, Richard Hugh De Courcy Stanesby, shrugged his shoulders scornfully.

"Evidently, Dick, that mail wasn't satisfactory. Has she clean forgot you, Dick, the little white mouse of a cousin, with the pretty blue eyes? She was mighty sweet on you, and————"

But there was a frown on Dick's usually good-tempered face. He was in no mind to take his old chum's pleasantry kindly, and the other saw it, and drew his own conclusions therefrom.

"Chucked him over, poor beggar, I suppose. Hang it all! Women are all alike; once a man's down, he's forgotten," but he did not speak his thoughts aloud. He looked away across the sweltering plain, and said casually,

"Where do you hang out, old man?"

Stanesby pointed east in a vague sort of manner, that might indicate South Australia, or far distant New South Wales.

"Got a shanty on the creek there," he said laconically.

"Creek, is there a creek? The place looks as if it hadn't seen water since the beginning of the world."

"Oh, there's a creek right enough. I believe it's a big one when it rains, but it hasn't rained since I 've been here, and there ain't much water in it. Just a little in the hole opposite the hut. The niggers say its permanent. Springs, or something of that sort."

"Niggers! That's what I 've come over about. They've worried the life out of us on Jinfalla. Taken to spearing the cattle, and the men too if they get a chance. Old Anderson thinks we ought to have some 'concerted action,' and settle the matter once for all."

"H'm. Wipe 'em out, I suppose he means?"

"It's what a squatter generally means, isn't it, when he talks about the blacks? Sounds brutal, but hang it all, man, what the devil is a fellow to do? They 're only beasts, and as beasts you must treat 'em. Look here, there was a young fellow on our run, as nice a boy as you 'd wish to see—his people were something decent at home, I believe, but the lad had got into some scrape and cleared out, and drifted along into the heart of Western Australia here. He was riding tracks for old Anderson about two hundred miles to the west there. He didn't come in last week for his tucker, so they sent word for me to look him up."

"Well?" for Turner paused, and drew a long breath.

"Well—same old nip, of course. His hut was burnt, and he and his hutkeeper—I tell you, Dick, it won't bear talking about—he was a lad of twenty, and the hutkeeper was an old lag, might have been seventy to look at him, but when I found their bodies down by the creek, I couldn't tell which was which."

"It's bad," said Stanesby, "very bad. What did you do?"

"Buried 'em, of course, my mate and I, and shot the first buck we came across skulking in the bush. What would you have us do?"

"It's all bad together," said the other man, with an oath. "The blacks about here are tame enough if you let 'em alone, but these young fellows get meddling with their women, and—well——"

"That 's all very well, but you didn't find a mate too ghastly a corpse to look at, or you wouldn't take the matter so coolly. You 'd have done just as I did. Something must be done, old man, or the country won't be habitable."

They had been riding along slowly, side by side, one man eager, anxious, interested, the other evidently with his thoughts far away. The mail he had got that morning was stuffed into his saddlebags, and the news it brought him made him think longingly of a home in far-away England, a creeper-covered house, and a cosy room with a bright fire, and the rain beating pleasantly on the windows. Rain—he had not seen rain for three long years. Always the hard blue sky and the bright sunshine, always the dreary plain, broken here and there by patches of prickly bush and still more thorny spinifex, always the red bluffs marking the horizon, clean cut against the cloudless sky.

Habitable? Such a country as this habitable? It had given him bread for the last three years, but—but—he felt burning in his pocket the letter summoning him home—telling of the death, the unexpected death, of his young cousin, that made him master of that pleasant home, that filled his empty pockets. What did anyone ever dream of living in such a country for—driving the unlucky niggers back and back? What need for it? What need? Far better leave it to the niggers, and clear out altogether.

Had Gladys forgotten? He wondered. The little white mouse of a cousin, as Turner called her, who had cried so bitterly when he left, and even now answered his letters so regularly, those letters that had come to be written at longer and longer intervals as home ties weakened, and the prospect of seeing her again slowly died away. Had she forgotten—had she? She looked like the sort of woman that would be faithful—faithful—well, as faithful as any one in this world could be expected to be, as faithful as women always are to their lovers in distant lands. Turner had been sweet there once too, curious he should meet him just now; he had forgotten her surely, or he would never have referred to her so casually. Yes, Turner had forgotten, and yet he had been very bad too—strange how completely a thing like that passes out of a man's life. Could he take up the broken threads just where he left off—could he? So sweet and tender as she was, so quiet and restful. There was that other one, who loved him after her fashion too, but—pah, it was an insult to Gladys to name her in the same breath—she—she—The country was not habitable—a doghole unfit for a European; what was Turner making such a song over the niggers for?

"Old man," said Turner, he had been telling to unlistening ears the tale of how the blacks had speared, in wanton mischief, a mob of two hundred cattle on Jinfalla, not fifteen miles from the home station, "old man, you see it would be just ruination to let this go on. Either they or we must clear out. We can't both live here, that's certain."

"Always the same old yarn wherever the Englishman goes, always the same old yarn. Poor niggers!"

"Well, what'd you have?" said the other warmly; "something's got to be done."

"I 'm going to cut it all."

"What?" Turner stopped his horse and looked his companion full in the face. "Cut it all?"

"My cousin 's dead."

"John Stanesby?"

"John Stanesby."

"And Heyington 's yours?"

"And Eastwood too."

"Good Lord!"

There was silence for a moment. Then Turner said again:

"You can marry Gladys Rowan now."

"Yes."

Then he added, as if as an afterthought, "If she 'll have me."

"No fear of that," said Turner with a sigh. Then he turned to his old chum, and stretching over laid a kindly hand on his arm, "I congratulate you, old chap."

"Thank you." And they rode on in silence, the one man thinking bitterly that if ever he had cherished a spark of hope of winning the woman he had loved he must give it up at last, the other trying to realise the good fortune that had come to him.

And an hour ago he had been as this man beside him—only one little hour ago!

"How far do you reckon it to the head-station? Fifty miles?"

"Fifty? Nearer eighty I should say."

"Then I guess I 'll put up at your place. How far's that?"

"About ten miles."

"All right. Lead on, master of Heyington."

To refuse a man hospitality in the bush—such a thing was never heard of, and, though Stanesby said no welcoming word, it never occurred to Turner to doubt that he was more than welcome.

"It's right out of your way."

Turner stared.

"Good Lord! What's ten miles, and we haven't met for years. I must say, old chap, you don't seem particularly pleased to see an old chum."

"I—they ain't so plentiful I can afford to do that. No, I was thinking of going in to the station with you."

"Right you are, old man, do you? Only we'll put up at your place for the night—my horse's pretty well done—and go on in the morning."

Stanesby said nothing, only turned his horse's head slightly to the left. Save the red bluffs away to the east there was nothing to mark the change of direction. There was no reason apparently for his choosing one direction rather than another.

They rode in silence, these two who had been college chums and had not met for years. Possibly it was the one man's good fortune that raised a barrier between them. It was not easy for Turner to talk of present difficulties and troubles when, as Stanesby said, he was going to "cut it all"; it was not easy for him to speak of bygone times when the other man was going back to them, and he would be left here without a prospect of a change. And Stanesby said nothing, he could only think of the great difference between them; and yesterday there was nothing he would have liked better than this meeting with his old friend, which to-day fell flat. No, he had nothing to say. Already their paths lay wide apart.

An hour's slow riding brought them to the creek Stanesby had spoken of. There was no gentle slope down to the river, the plain simply seemed to open at their feet, and show them the river bed some twenty feet below. Only a river bed about twenty yards wide, but there was no water to be seen, only signs, marked signs in that thirsty land, that water had been there. Down where the last moisture had lingered the grass grew green and fresh, and leafy shrubs and small trees and even tangled creepers made this dip in the plain a pleasant resting-place for the eye wearied with the monotony of the world above it.

"By Jove!" cried Turner, surprised.

"Told you so," said his companion, "but it ain't much after all. Fancy calling that wiry stuff grass in England, and admiring those straggly creepers and shrubs. Why we wouldn't give 'em house-room in the dullest, deadest corner of the wilderness at home."

"Lucky beggar!" sighed the other man. "But you see they 're all I 'm likely to have for many a long year to come. Hang it all, man, I bet you 'd put that shrub there, that chap with the bright red flower, into your hot-house and look after him with the greatest care, or your gardener would for you."

"It'd require a d——d hot house," said Stanesby laconically, wiping his hot face.

They did not descend into the bed of the creek, the ground was better adapted for riding up above, and a mile further along they came upon a large blackfellows' camp stretched all along the edge of a water-hole.

"The brutes," said Turner; "bagging the water of course."

"They 'd die if they didn't, I suppose. This, and the hole by my place is the only water I know of for forty miles round. After all they were here first, and if I had my way they'd be left to it."

"All very well for you to talk," grumbled Turner. "Do they look worth anything?"

Certainly they did not. The camp was a mere collection of breakwinds made of bark and branches, more like badly-stacked woodheaps than anything else, and the children of the soil lay basking in the sun, among the dogs and filth and refuse of the camp, or crouched over small fires as if it were bitter cold.

The dogs started up yelping, for a blackfellow's dog doesn't know how to bark properly, as the white men passed, but their masters took no notice. A stark naked gin, with a fillet of greasy skin bound round her head, and a baby slung in a net on her back, came whining to Turner with outstretched hands. She had mixed with the stockkeepers before, and knew a few words of English.

"Give it terbacker along a black Mary. Budgery{1} fellow you," but he pushed her away with the butt end of his whip.

"My place's not above a mile away now," said Stanesby, as they left the precincts of the camp behind them.

"I wouldn't have those beggars so close, if I were you. Some fine morning you'll find yourself—"

"Pooh! They're quite tame and harmless. I 've got a boy from them about the place, and he's very good as boys go. Besides, I 'm off as soon as possible."

1 Means "good."

"Well, I bet you the man who takes your place thinks differently."

"Very likely."

"Got a decent hutkeeper?"

"What? Oh yes. Pretty fair."

Clearly Stanesby was not in the mood for conversation, and Turner gave it up as a bad job. It was about two o'clock now, the very hottest hour of the day, and all nature seemed to feel it. Not a sound broke the stillness, not the cry of bird or beast, nothing save the sound of their horses' hoofs on the hard ground was to be heard.

"By Jove!" said Turner, "this is getting unbearable. I vote we get down and shelter for a spell under the lee of the bank."

For all answer, Stanesby raised his whip and pointed ahead.

"There 's the hut," he said. "Better get on."

It was hardly distinguishable from the surrounding plain, the little hut built of rough logs, and roofed with sheets of bark stripped from the trees which grew in the river-bed. Down in the creek there was a waterhole, a waterhole surrounded by tall reeds and other aquatic vegetation which gave it a look of permanence, of freshness and greenness in this burnt-up land. But that was down in the creek, round the hut was the plain, barren here as elsewhere; no effort had been made to cultivate it or improve it, and the desert came up to the very doors. The only sign of human life was the refuse from the small household—an empty tin or two, fragments of broken bottles, and scraps of rag and paper, only that and the hut itself, and a small yard for horses and cattle, that was all—not a tree, not a green thing. The bed of the creek was their garden, but it was not visible from the house; its inmates could only see the desolate plain, nothing but that for miles and miles, far as the eye could see. So monotonous, so dreary an outlook, it was hardly possible to believe there was anything else in the world, anything but this lonely little hut, with, for all its paradise, the waterhole in the creek below.

Turner said nothing. It was exactly what he expected; he lived in a similar place, a place without a creek close handy, where the only water came from a well, and undiluted, was decidedly unpleasant to the taste. No, in his eyes Stanesby had nothing to grumble at.

The owner of this palatial residence coo-eed shrilly.

"Jimmy; I say, Jimmy!"

A long, lank black boy, clad in a Crimean shirt and a pair of old riding breeches, a world too big for him, rose lazily up from beside the house, where he had been basking in the sun, and came towards them.

Stanesby dismounted and flung him his reins, Turner following suit.

"All gone sleep," said Jimmy, nodding his head in the direction of the hut, a grin showing up the white of his regular teeth against his black face.

"Come on in, Turner."

The door was open and the two men walked straight into the small hut.

It was very dark at first coming in out of the brilliant sunshine, but as Turner's eyes grew accustomed to the light, he saw that the interior was just exactly what he should have expected it to be. The floor was hard earth, the walls were unlined, the meagre household goods were scattered about in a way that did not say much for his friend's hutkeeper, a shelf with a few old books and papers on it, was the only sign of culture, and a rough curtain of sacking dividing the place in two, was the only thing that was not common to every hut in all that part of Western Australia.

"Howling swell, you are, old chap! Go in for two rooms I see."

The curtain was thrust aside, and to Turners astonishment, a girl's face peered round it. A beautiful girl's face too, the like of which he had not seen for many a year, if indeed, he had ever seen one like it before; a face with oval, liquid dark eyes in whose depths a light lay hidden, with full red pouting lips, and a broad low brow half hidden by heavy masses of dark, untidy hair, which fell in picturesque confusion over it. A beautiful face in shape and form, and rich dark colouring, and Turner started back too astonished to speak. Such a face! Never in all his life had he seen such a face, and the look turned on his companion was easy enough to read.

"Come here, Kitty," said Stanesby in an unconcerned voice. "I want some dinner for this gentleman."

Then she stepped out, and the illusion vanished. For she was only a half-caste, beautiful as a dream, or he who had not seen a woman for many a long day—he never counted the black gins women—thought so, but only a despised half-caste, outcast both from father's and mother's race.

Not that she looked unhappy. On the contrary, she came forward and smiled on him a slow, lazy smile, the smile of one who is utterly contented with her lot in life.

"Whew! So that 's our hutkeeper, is it?"

"Dinner, Kitty."

The girl took a tin dish from the shelf and went outside. She walked well and gracefully, and Turner followed her with his eyes.

"By Jove!" he said, "talk about good looks. Why, Dick, you—"

"Hang it all, man," said Stanesby. "I know well enough what you 're thinking. The girl *is* good-looking, I suppose, for a half-caste. The boss's sister, old Miss Howard, found her among the tribe, a wild little wretch, and took her in and did her best to civilise her; but it wasn't easy work, and the old lady died before it was done."

"And you 're completing the job?"

Stanesby shrugged his shoulders.

"I saw her, of course, when I went in to the head-station, which wasn't very often, and I suppose I told her she was a good-looking girl. She mayn't understand much, but she understood *that* right enough, trust a woman for that. Good Lord! I never gave her a second thought, till I found her at my door one night. The little beggar had had a row with 'em up at the house and came right off to me. It wasn't any use protesting. She might have done worse, and here she 's been ever since. But she's got the temper of a fiend, I can tell you, and it ain't all skittles and beer."

The girl entered the room and Stanesby began turning over his mail letters, making his companion feel that the subject had better be dropped between them. He had explained the girl's presence, he wanted no comments from his old friend.

He filled his pipe and sat down on the only three-legged stool the hut contained, watching his friend seated on a box opposite and the girl passing in and out getting ready the rough meal. She was graceful, she was beautiful, as some wild thing is beautiful, there was no doubt whatever of that. Her dress was of Turkey red; old Miss Howard had had a fancy for dressing all her dark *protegées* in bright colours, and they had followed in her footsteps up at the station, and Turner mentally appraising the girl before him, quite approved her taste. The dress was old and somewhat faded, but its severe simplicity and its dull tints just set off the girl's dusky beauty. Shoes and stockings she had none, but what matter? any touch of civilisation would have spoiled the picture.

Stanesby apparently took no notice of her, but began to read extracts from his letters and papers for his companion's benefit. He was hardly at his ease, and Turner made only a pretence of listening. He could not take his eyes from the girl who was roughly setting out the table for their meal. "The temper of a fiend," truly he thought it not unlikely, judging by the glances she threw at him whenever she took her eyes from Stanesby. She could hardly have understood what he read, but she listened intently and cast angry glances every now and then on Turner. He and these letters, she seemed to feel, were not of her world, they were taking this man away from her. Yes, he could well believe she had the temper of a fiend. But she said nothing. Her mother had come of a race which from time immemorial had held its women in bondage, and she spoke no word, probably she had no words in which to express her feelings.

The table was laid at last, and a piece of smoking salt beef and a great round damper brought in from outside and put on it.

"Dinner," said the girl sullenly, but Stanesby went on reading, and paid no attention, and Turner felt himself watching to see what would happen next. He caught only snatches of the letter, just enough to know it was a description of a hunt in England, of a damp, cold, cloudy day, of an invigorating run—the contrast struck him forcibly—the stifling, hot little hut, and the jealous, half-savage woman standing there, her eyes aflame with anger at the slight she fancied was put upon her.

She stole over and touched Stanesby lightly on the arm, but he shook her off as he would a fly and went on reading calmly.

The other man watched the storm gather on her face. She stood for one moment looking, not at Stanesby but at him; it was very evident whom she blamed for her lover's indifference; then she stretched across to the table and caught up a knife. Her breath was coming thick and fast and Turner never took his eyes off her, in between her gasping breath he heard his friend's voice, slow and deliberate as ever, still telling the tale of the English hunting day, still reading the letter which put such a world between him and the girl standing beside him. Then there was a flash of steel, Turner felt rather than saw that it was directed at him, and, before he even had time to think, Stanesby had sprung to his feet and grasped her by the arm.

"Would you now? Would you?" He might have been speaking to a fractious horse. Then as Turner too sprang to his feet and snatched the knife from her hand, he flung her off with an oath.

"You little devil!" He sat down again with an uneasy laugh, and the girl with an inarticulate cry flung herself out of the open door. In all the half hour that had elapsed, she had spoken no word except when she called them to their dinner; but in that inarticulate moan the other man seemed to read the whole bitterness of her story.

"I told you," said Stanesby, he seemed to feel some explanation or apology were necessary; "I told you she had the temper of a fiend. I hope she didn't hurt you, old man?"

"No, no. She meant business, though, only you were too quick for her. But I say, old man, it isn't well to have a good-looking young woman fix her affections on you in that ardent manner. There'll be the devil to pay, some day."

The other laughed, and then sighed.

"I tell you it was no fault of mine," he said.

"Come on and get something to eat. There's whisky in that bottle."

Virtually he had dismissed the subject; with the disappearance of the girl he would have let the matter drop, but he was not at his ease, and his old chum was less so. It was all very well to talk of old times, of college days, of mutual friends, each was thinking, and each was uncomfortably conscious that the other, too, was thinking, of that dark-eyed, straight-limbed young savage who had forced her personality upon them both, and was so far, so very far, removed from the world of which they spoke. There was another thing too, a fair-haired, blue-eyed girl, as different—as different as the North Pole from the Equator—each had loved her, to each she had been the embodiment of all earthly virtues, and each thought of her as well, too—the one man bitterly. Why should this man, this whilom friend of his, have everything? And the other man read his thoughts, and unreasoning anger grew up in his heart against his old chum. It has nothing whatever to do with Dick Stanesby's hutkeeper, of course, nothing whatever; but it is nevertheless a fact, that these two old friends spent what should have been a pleasant afternoon, devoted to reminiscences of old times and a renewal of early friendship, in uncomfortable silence. The monthly mail, which Stanesby had brought in, contained many papers, and after their meal they lighted their pipes and read diligently, first one paper and then another. At first they made efforts at conversation, read out incidents and scraps of news and commented thereon, but as the afternoon wore on, the silence grew till it became difficult to break it. The sunlight outside crept in and in through the open doorway. There were no shadows because there was nothing to cast shadows, save the banks of the creek down below the level of the plain and the red bluffs, thirty miles to the eastward. But the sun stole in and crossed the hard earthen floor, and stole up the wall on the other side, crept up slowly, emphasising the dull blankness of the place. So did the sun every day of the year, pretty nearly; so did he in every stockkeeper's hut on the plains of Western Australia; but to-day he seemed to Turner to be mocking his misery, pointing it out and emphasising it. Such his life had been for the last three or four years; such it was now; such it would be to the end. He could see no prospect of change, no prospect of better things: always the bare walls and the earthen floors for him; unloved, uncared for he had lived, unloved and uncared for he would die. And this man beside him—bah! it would not bear thinking of. He pushed back the stool he had been sitting on, and strolling to the door looked out. Nothing in sight but the black boy, who wasn't a boy at all, but a man apparently over thirty years of age, lolling up against the verandah post, like one who had plenty of time on his hands.

Stanesby got up and joined him. The hot wind that had blown fiercely all day had died down, and now there hardly seemed a breath of air stirring. It was stupid to comment on the weather in a place where the weather was always the same, but Turner felt the need of something to say, so he seized on the well-worn topic.

"It's getting a little cooler, I think."

"Confound it, no."

Stanesby looked round discontentedly. The untidy, uninviting remains of their midday meal were still on the table, pushed aside to make room for the papers they had been reading; it gave the place a dishevelled, comfortless air, which made its dull blank-ness ten times worse.

Turner noticed it, but he did not feel on sufficiently good terms to rail at his friend's hutkeeper, as he would have done in the morning. He only shrugged his shoulders meaningly when Stanesby called out,

"Boy! I say, Jimmy, where's the girl?"

Jimmy turned lazily and showed his white teeth.

"Sit down along a creek, you bet."

"Go and fetch her."

Jimmy showed his white teeth again, and grinned largely, but he did not stir.

"My word! Baal{1} this blackfellow go."

"Much as his life is worth, I guess," said

1 *Means "not, no."*

Turner grimly, "judging by the specimen of her temper the young lady gave us this afternoon."

Stanesby muttered something that was hardly a blessing under his breath, then he caught up his hat and went down the bank to the waterhole. The other man felt more comfortable in his absence. He sat down, lighted his pipe, and taking up the paper again, began to read with fresh interest.

Half an hour passed. The sun sank below the horizon, gorgeous in red and gold, and Turner watched the last rosy flush die out of the western sky. Darkness fell, and he sat on smoking and thinking sadly, till his comrade loomed up out of the gloom.

"Is that you, Stanesby?" he called out.

"Who the devil should it be?" Then remembering his hospitality, "Why you Ye all in the dark! Why didn't you light a candle!"

The girl did not make her appearance, and Turner did not comment on her absence. Stanesby said nothing. He lighted a candle, and calling Jimmy to his assistance, began clearing the table and washing up the dirty plates and pannikins. Turner offered to help, but was told ungraciously that two were enough, and so went on smoking and watched in silence. He did not feel on intimate enough terms to comment; but he knew well enough Stanesby had gone out to find the girl, and either failed to find her, or at any rate failed to bring her back. It was no business of his any way, and he sat smoking till he was called to the evening meal, which was a repetition of the mid-day one, with milkless tea instead of whisky for a beverage.

Stanesby apologised.

"I 'm clean out of whisky, I 'm sorry to say."

"It's all right, old man. I don't often manage to get it at all on Jinfalla."

They discussed station matters then, discussed them all the evening, though Turner could not but feel that his host's thoughts were far away. Still they lasted, they interested the man who was bound to live on here, till at length Stanesby got up with a mighty yawn and suggested they should turn in.

There was a bunk fixed against the wall, and he threw his comrade's blankets into it.

"It's all I can do for you to-night, old man. Come to Heyington next year, and I 'll treat you better."

"Thanks," said Turner. "No such luck for me." Then he spoke the thought that had been in his mind all the evening.

"I say, that girl hasn't come in."

"She's all right, she can sleep out then. I can't say it'll cool her temper, for it's as hot as blazes still. Good night, old chap."

Turner lay awake long after the light was out, staring up at the unceiled roof, at the faint light that marked the open doorway and the window, thinking, thinking, wondering at his own discontent, thinking of the fair-haired, blue-eyed girl he had loved so well and so long. It was all over between them now, all over; there had never been anything except on his side, never anything at all, and now it was not much good his even thinking of her. She would marry Dick Stanesby and never know, never dream——

His thoughts wandered to that other girl, it was no business of his, but it worried him nevertheless, as things that are no concern of ours do worry us when we lie wakeful on our beds, and the *girl's* beautiful, angry face haunted him. He thought of her there down by the creek, alone in her dumb pain, so young, so ignorant, so beautiful. There was something wrong in the scheme of creation somewhere, something wrong, or why were such as she born but to suffer. His life was hard, cruelly hard, he had known better things; but she—she—hers had been hard all along. Had she known any happiness? he wondered. He supposed she had if she cared for Dick Stanesby. When first she came, unasked and unsought, he had been good to her; he knew his friend, he had known him from a boy, easy-going, good-natured, with no thought for the future for himself, how could he expect him to think for another? He had been good to her—oh, yes, he knew Dick Stanesby—very good to her, but he had taken no thought for her future any more than he would for his own. He would go into the head-station with him to-morrow morning, he very much doubted if he would come back. He would intend to at first, but it would be very much easier to stay, and he would stay, and the girl—what would become of her? He found himself saying it over and over again to himself, what would become of her? What could become of her? till he fell into an uneasy doze and dreamed that he was master of Heyington and had married Gladys Rowan, who was no other than Dick Stanesby's hutkeeper, and crouched in the corner with a long, shining knife in her hand. Then he awakened suddenly and heard the sound of voices, a woman's voice and Dick's, Dick's soft and tender. He could not hear the words, but the tones were enough. It was the same old Dick. He did not want her, he would rather be without her: but since she was there, he must needs be good to her. So she had come back after all! He might have known she was sure to come back. Why couldn't she stop away? Why couldn't she join her relatives down by the creek? Alas! and alas! The barrier between her and them was as great as it was between her and the white man. Greater, if possible. Poor child! poor child! How was it to end?

He tossed and turned and the voices went on softly murmuring. He thought of Gladys and grew angry, and finally, when he had given up all hope, he fell fast asleep.

Next morning he found that peace reigned. The girl came in and quietly cleared away the remnants of last night's meal and began making preparations for breakfast. Her mind was at ease evidently. She had no doubts about the permanency of her heaven; and when she saw him she smiled upon him the same slow, lazy, contented smile with which she had first greeted him, apparently forgetting and expecting him to forget all disagreeable episodes of the day before. How long would this peace last? asked Guy Turner of himself.

The meal done, Stanesby called to his black boy to bring up the horses, and touching the girl on the shoulder drew her aside, evidently to explain that he was going into the head-station and wanted provisions for the journey.

"We'll take a packhorse between us," said he to Turner, "it'll save trouble; and I 'll show you a decent camping-place for to-night." Then he followed the girl outside, and his companion began rolling up his swag.

He came back a few moments later, the girl following, and Turner could not but note the change in her face. It was not angry now, there was hardly even a trace of sullenness on it. Fear and sorrow seemed struggling with one another for the upper hand, and she was sobbing every now and then heavily, as if she could not help herself.

"Good Lord! Stanesby, what the dickens have you been doing to the girl?" he said.

Stanesby looked at him angrily.

"You seem to take a confoundedly big interest in the girl," he said.

"Well, hang it all, man, she looks as if she had been having a jolly bad time, and really she's only a child."

"A child, is she? A child that's very well able to take care of herself. I haven't been beating her, if that's what you 're thinking. I suppose I may be allowed to go into the head-station occasionally without asking my hutkeeper's leave."

"Oh! that's the trouble, is it? Depends upon your hutkeeper, I should say. I don't ask mine, but then—"

Turner paused, and Stanesby answered the unspoken thoughts with an oath.

"Oh, if you feel that way," began Turner, but his companion flung himself out of the hut angrily.

Then the girl turned round, and Turner wondered to himself if she were going to repeat the performance of last night. But no, she was quiet and subdued now, as if all hope, all resentment even, had left her.

"Going to the head station?" she asked, and her voice was soft and low and very sweet, with just a trace of the guttural enunciation of her mother's race; but she spoke good English, far better than her appearance seemed to warrant, and did no small credit to old Miss Howard's training.

"Yes, yes, of course. We're going to the head station, but Stanesby 'll be back in a day or two," he added soothingly, because of the sorrow on her face. And then he hated himself for saying so much. What business was it of his?

She stepped forward and laid both hands on his arm.

"Don't take him away, don't, don't!" she pleaded.

Her big dark eyes were swimming with tears, and there was an intensity of earnestness in her tones that went to the young man's heart. Besides, he was young, and she was very good to look upon.

"My dear child," he said, his anger against his old friend growing, "I have nothing in the world to do with it. He must go into the head-station sometimes. He must have gone often before."

She dropped her hands and leaned back wearily against the wall.

"No," she said, "no, not when the myalls are down along the creek."

"Good Lord! Those d——d black fellows! I never thought of them. But they won't touch you!"

She looked up and smiled faintly, as if amused at his ignorance.

"Kitty tumble down," she said, relapsing into the blackfellows' English.

"Oh! come, I say," said Turner, "this'll never do." And he went outside in search of Stanesby, whom he found strapping their swags on to the packhorse.

"Look here, I say, old man, that poor little beggar's frightened out of her wits of the myalls down by the creek there."

Stanesby shrugged his shoulders.

"All bunkum! I know her ways. She wants to get me to stop. She seems to guess there's something in the wind. The myalls! pooh! They 're as tame as possible. They steal any odds and ends that are left about—that's about their form."

"But the poor child is frightened."

"Frightened! Get out. There wasn't much fright about her when she took the knife to you last night! She knows very well how to take care of herself, I can tell you."

"But those myalls. On Jinfalla we—Well, it really seems to me risky to leave her all alone. Even if there isn't any danger—the very fact of being alone—."

"Pooh! Considering she tramped from the head-station here all the eighty miles on foot, just because of some breeze with the cook there, she must be mightily afraid of being alone. However, if you don't like her being left, it 's open to you to stop and look after her. I 'm going to start in about two minutes."

"Oh, well, if you think it s all right—"

"Of course it's all right. There 's Jimmy got your horse for you. Come on, old chap."

Turner mounted, and Stanesby was just about to do the same, when with a quick cry the girl ran out of the hut and caught his arm.

She said no word, and before he, taken by surprise, could stop her, she had wound both her arms around his neck and laid her face against his breast.

Turner put his spurs into his horse, and rode off smartly. It was no affair of his. The whole thing made him angry whenever he thought of it.

As for Dick Stanesby, though usually never anything but gentle with a woman, he was thoroughly angry now; he had felt angry before, but now he was roused, which did not often happen, to put his anger into words.

"Confound you, Kitty! Do you hear me? Don't be a fool!" and he roughly shook her off, so roughly that she lost her balance, staggered, and fell. He made a step forward to take his horse, which was held by the stolid black boy, but she was too quick for him and, grovelling on the ground at his feet, put out her arms and held him there, murmuring inarticulate words of tenderness and love. Stanesby stooped down, and caught her wrists in both his hands.

"Get up!" he said roughly, and dragged her to her feet. She stood there, leaning all her weight on his supporting hands, looking at him with reproachful eyes.

They were beautiful eyes, and there was need enough for her sorrow had she only known; but what Stanesby was thinking of was the awkwardness of the situation. He did not mind the black boy, he counted him as so much dirt— but Turner! Already this girl had made an exhibition of him, and now it was worse than ever. Every moment he dreaded he would turn round, and even though he did not it was equally bad, he kept his face purposely averted.

The girl broke out into passionate prayer to him not to leave her, then, seeing he was still unmoved, she began to call him every tender name her limited vocabulary contained, though there was little enough need to do that, her eyes said enough.

"Kitty, go back to the hut this moment! For God's sake, don't be such a fool! One would think I was going to murder you."

"The myalls will," she said. Then she paused, and added solemnly, "to-morrow."

"What confounded rot!"

He let go her hands suddenly, and she fell to her knees and tried to put her arms round him again; but with a quick movement he stepped backwards, and she fell forward on to her face. He pushed her aside roughly, angrily, with an anger that was not all against her, and mounted hurriedly, snatched the packhorse's rein from the black boy, and was off at full gallop after his friend before she could regain her feet But she did not try to, once she realised that all hope was gone. He had left her, it was all over with her, she might just as well lie there.

At the sound of the galloping horses behind him Turner looked round. Through the haze of the early morning, the haze that promised fierce heat later on, he saw the horses coming towards him, and beyond, half-veiled by the dust they made as they passed, a dusky red bundle flung carelessly out on the plain, of use to no one. The black boy walked away, it was no business of his. There was the lonely hut and the far-reaching plain, nothing in sight but the bluffs far away to the east, nothing at all, only that red bundle lying there alone and neglected.

He had no words for his comrade when he did come up. That dusky red heap seemed to fill all his thoughts, and about that silence was best. Stanesby checked his horses, and they rode on slowly as men who have a long journey before them. The sun climbed up and up to the zenith, but there was no shelter, no place for the noonday rest. Then away in the distance arose a line of trees raised up above the horizon, and Stanesby pointed it out to his companion.

"We can spell there a bit," he said. "It's only that beastly prickly bush, for all it looks like a forest of red gum at the very least from here, but there'll be a scrap of shade, and I'm getting tired. There's water there sometimes, but it was dry as a bone last time I passed."

"It's a grand country!" sighed Turner.

"By George!" said Stanesby, "I never will come back this way. Why should I, now I 'm free to do as I please?"

Why, indeed? And Turner's thoughts immediately flew back to the dark-eyed girl, and the solitary hut as he had last seen it through the haze of the morning, with that red heap lying there carelessly flung aside, and the black fellow stalking away. Why should he go back? Why indeed? Only to have that scene repeated. Better go straight on to England, and home, and pretty, fair-haired, blue-eyed Gladys Rowan.

So they lay there in the scanty shade and spelled, and built a small fire of dry sticks, and filled the billy from the waterbag that hung at each horse's neck, and boiled their tea, and ate their humble mid-day meal, and dozed the afternoon away, lazily watching the hobbled horses as they searched on the still damp edges of the shallow clay pan for such scanty grass as the moisture induced to grow there. They hardly spoke, they had nothing in common now; once they reached the head-station, they would part never to meet again. Each felt it instinctively, and each was thankful that it should be so. The sooner the parting came, the better now.

The shadows of the thorny bushes began to grow longer and longer as the sun sank in the west, and they mounted their horses and started off again. Then the sun went down, and the colour faded out of the sky as the stars, bright points of light, came out one by one. The new moon was a silver rim clear cut in the west, and not a sound broke the stillness. How lonely it was, how intensely lonely! Turner thought of the poor girl alone in the hut miles behind them, and wondered if his companion too were thinking of her. After all, surely the very loneliness gave safety. At any rate, she was safe at night. If the blacks did not attack at dusk they would leave her alone for the night. But the morning—next morning! Was it right to leave her? He himself had no faith in the myall blacks, they were treacherous, they were cruel. Had he not come over to arrange some plan of campaign against them? And yet he went away and left that girl at their mercy, completely at their mercy. He felt strongly tempted to turn back. If they could not stop with her, at least they might have brought her along with them. She was defenceless; her blood was no protection, rather the reverse. And then, when he turned to speak to

Stanesby, the recollection of his scornful, "It's open to you to stop and look after her," tied his tongue. After all, it was not likely Stanesby would have left if there was the slightest danger; he had lived among these blacks, he understood them thoroughly; it was an insult to the man he had known all his life to suppose anything else; and yet the thought of the girl's loneliness haunted him. The moon set, and by the starlight they saw looming up ahead some rocks, isolated rocks, roughly piled together by some giant hand.

"We'll camp there," said Stanesby, "there's a little water down under the rocks—about enough to keep life in the horses; there's some grass and a bush or two to make a fire. What more could the heart of man desire?"

Out in the bush not much time is wasted, and soon after they had halted their blankets were spread, and they were asleep, or lying, if not asleep, staring up at the bright starlit sky of the southern hemisphere.

But Turner could not sleep, it was worse than it had been the night before. Why should he be haunted in this way? Why should he take Stanesby's sins on his shoulders? The girl was all right, she must be all right; why should she haunt his dreams, and keep him wakeful on his hard bed, when he had a long journey still before him? Stanesby was sleeping peacefully as a child. He could hear his deep breathing; if there was anything to be feared he would not sleep like that. It was hot still, very hot. This was an awful climate, a cruel life, and Stanesby had done with it all. No wonder he slept soundly.

He sat up restlessly. A sound in the distance broke the stillness, then he started, surely it was the trotting of a horse. He rubbed his eyes. Their own three horses were there close beside them, he could see them vague and indistinct in the gloom. They were there right enough. What could this be? Who could be riding about at this time of night? They were still a good forty miles from the head-station, and this horse was coming from the opposite direction.

He put out his hand, and shook his companion awake.

"Some one's coming," he said shortly.

"Some one! Gammon! Good Lord!—"

There was no doubt about it, and he rose to his feet It was the other side of the rocks, and they walked round quietly. They were only curious, there was nothing to fear. In the dim starlight they saw a man on horseback advancing towards them.

"Hallo!" called out Stanesby, as he came quite close, "who the devil are you?"

The horse was done. They could hear his gasping breath, and the man bent forward as if he too had come far and fast, but he did not answer, and as he came closer Turner saw he was a blackfellow.

Stanesby saw it too, and saw more, for he recognised his own black boy Jimmy.

"Good God! Jimmy, is it you?"

There must be something wrong, very wrong indeed, that would bring a black-fellow, steeped in superstitious fears of demons and evil spirits, out at dead of night.

"Jimmy!" Stanesby caught him by the shoulder, and fairly pulled him from his horse, "What's the meaning of this?"

Jimmy did not answer for a moment. He was occupied with his horse's bridle, then he said carelessly, as if he were rather ashamed of making such a fuss about a trifle.

"Myalls pull along a hut."

"My God!" cried Turner. It seemed like the realisation of his worst fears.

But Stanesby refused to see any cause for alarm.

"And you 've ridden like blazes, and ruined the mare, to tell us rot like that. What if they do come up to the hut? They've been there before."

The answer was more to his companion than his servant, but Jimmy answered the implied reproach.

"Blackfellow burn hut," he stated.

"Nonsense!"

"This fellow sit down along a bush," he went on stolidly.

"Well—if you did! I wish to heaven you had stopped alongside your confounded bush before you ruined my mare."

"Bungally you!" said Jimmy, who was no respecter of persons, meaning "you are very stupid." "Blackfellow put firestick in humpy and—"

"Good God! Stanesby, I knew it. The myalls are going to burn down the hut, and this beggar's got wind of it."

Jimmy nodded approvingly.

"All gone humpy," he said, stretching out his hands as if to denote the deed was done.

"But the girl, Jimmy, the girl!"

"Poor gin tumble down."

"I—Jimmy," Stanesby caught him by the shoulder, and shook him violently, and Turner knew by the change in his voice that his fears were roused at last, "how did you know this? When did you hear it?"

"Sit down along a bush," said Jimmy again. His vocabulary was limited.

"But when—when? It must have been all right when you left?"

"Blackfellow pull along a humpy to-night," said Jimmy, nodding his head solemnly, feeling that at last he had got a serious hearing, and hoping to hear no more about the mare.

"But the girl—the girl! Where's the girl?"

"That one myall hit him gin along a cobra big fellow nulla-nulla? Gin tumble down." {1}

"But—my God! what 'd you leave her there for?"

"Myall got 'em nulla-nulla for this fellow."

"You brute!" cried Turner, "why didn't you bring her with you?"

"Only got 'em one yarramen," said the blackfellow nonchalantly. There was only one horse, he had taken it and saved his skin. He had come to warn the white man of the destruction of his dwelling, but he did not count the half-caste girl of any value one way or another. The blacks would attack the hut at sundown when they saw the coast clear.

   1 A blackfellow has hit the woman over the head with a big

   stick or club. The woman is dead.

The white man would be angry at the destruction of his hut, he had ridden after him to tell him, and also because safety lay with the white man; but the girl—if there had been a horse in the little paddock, he might possibly have brought her out of danger, but even as a blackfellow he looked with contempt on a half-caste; and as a woman—well, a woman was worth nothing as a woman. There were plenty more to be got. He lay down on the ground, and lazily stretched himself out at full length. There was nothing more to be got out of him.

Stanesby kicked him, and went for his horse.

"This is terrible!" he said, in a hoarse, husky whisper. "That poor child! Old man, I ought to have taken your advice. My God! Why did you let me leave her?"

Turner was saddling his own horse, and asking himself the self-same question. That girl's blood was on his head he felt, and yet—and yet—it was no business of his. Stanesby had declared all safe.

"What are you going to do?"

"Going straight back, of course."

"We'll be too late. Jimmy certainly said at sundown."

"He may be wrong, you know; besides, there's no trusting these devils. They might have changed their minds. You 'll help me, old man, won't you?"

"Of course."

It took but a few moments to prepare for that journey back. Each man saw that his revolvers were loaded, saddled his horse, and they were ready. The horse Jimmy had ridden was done.

"Shall we leave him?" said Stanesby, contemptuously stirring him with his foot.

"No, by Jove! no," said his companion, "we must have him. He knows all the sign."

So they forced the reluctant Jimmy to mount the packhorse, and distributed his load between them, taking only what was absolutely necessary.

When they were quite ready Stanesby looked at his watch.

"Ten o'clock," he said. "We must be there before daylight if we want to do any good;" and Turner could not but note that there was a more hopeful ring in his voice. Evidently he thought that perhaps all would be well after all.

They rode in silence, each man busy with his own thoughts. They had to ride judiciously too, for their horses were poor, and they had done forty miles already that day. Could they ever get back to the out-station before breakfast? Could they? And would they be in time if they did? Turner asked himself the question again and again, and he felt that his companion was doing the same thing. Whenever he touched his horse with the spur till the poor beast started forward with a fresh burst of energy, his companion felt he was thinking that the girl's life was forfeit by his carelessness, was wondering would they ever be in time.

Dawn would be about six o'clock. Forty miles to go, and eight hours to do it in. Forty miles straight ahead, with absolutely nothing to break the monotony except the little patch of prickly bush where they had spelled that afternoon. They went farther before they spelled to-night, and they did not stop then till it was very evident to both that the horses must have a rest, if it was only for half an hour. Turner lay on the ground and stared up at the starlit sky, and listened to the deep breathing of the black boy, and the restless pacing up and down of his companion. Then he fell into a doze from which he was aroused by Stanesby, and they were on their way again.

"We can't stop now till we get there," he said. "Old man, we must be in time. We must!"

But the other man said nothing. He could not judge, he could only hope. And now at the end of the journey, weary and tired, his hopes had gone down to zero.

The first faint streaks of dawn began to show themselves in the eastern sky, and Stanesby drew a long breath.

"My God! we Ye still a mile away."

"If they weren't there last night we'll be in time."

"Poor little girl! How thankful she 'll be to see us. It's all right, it must be all right."

And the light broadened in the east, the rosy light grew deeper and deeper, then it paled to bright gold, and behind, and all around, the world looked dark against that glowing light. Up came the rim of the sun, and Stanesby, urging his tired horse forward, said, "We ought to see the hut now. The confounded sun 's in my eyes."

Turner rubbed his own. But no, against the golden glowing rising sun the horizon was clean cut as ever, only the boundless plain, nothing more.

"Jimmy!" Stanesby's voice was sharp with pain and dread.

Jimmy raised his head sullenly. He was tired too, and considered himself ill-used.

"All gone humpy," he said.

Brighter and brighter grew the sunlight, another fierce hot day had begun. And there was nothing in sight, nothing. The plain was all around them, north, south, west, only in the east the red bluffs.

"All gone humpy." Their haste had been of no avail. The tale was told. They had come too late.

What need to ride for all they were worth now? But so they did ride, revolver in hand. And when they arrived at what had been Dick Stanesby's hut, an out-station of Nilpe Nilpe, there was nothing to mark it from the surrounding plain but a handful of ashes; even the hard earth showed no sign of trampling feet.

Stanesby flung himself off his horse like a madman.

"She may be all right. She must be all right. It may have been an accident. She is hidden down by the creek."

Turner said nothing. What could he say? His thoughts flew back to the lonely hut, and the girl lying there on the hard ground in her dusky red dress, alone, cast off, a thing of use to no one. Well, she was dead, he expected nothing else, and she was avenged. Surely this home-coming would haunt the man who had left her all the days of his life.

He laid his hand heavily on the black boy's shoulder.

"Track, you devil!"

And Jimmy led the way down towards the waterhole.

They followed him in silence.

The tall reeds looked green and fresh after the hot dry plain, but they also suggested another idea to Turner, and he tried to check his companion's headlong career.

"Look out! You don't know. They might be in those reed beds."

"All gone blackfellow," said Jimmy, and stolidly went ahead.

Then at last he brought them to what they sought. Dead, of course. Long before they started on that mad ride back her sufferings had been over. Dead! and Turner dared not look his companion in the face. No peace, no tenderness, about a death like this. It was too terrible! And this man had left her; in spite of her prayers he had left her!

They avenged her. The blacks had not gone far, but they could not follow them up that day. They spent it in the shade down by the waterhole, and Turner did not try to break his companion's silent reverie. Then when their horses were recruited they set out for the head-station of Nilpe Nilpe. There they told their tale. It was not much of a tale after all. Only a half-caste girl murdered, and a hut burnt. Such things happen every day. But the blacks must be punished, nevertheless, and half-a-dozen men rode out to do it, Stanesby at their head.

He was very silent. They said at the station, coming into a fortune had made him stuck-up and too proud to speak to a fellow, only Turner put a different construction on his silence. And the vengeance he took was heavy. They rode down among that tribe at bright noonday, led by Stanesby's black boy, who had been one of themselves, and when evening fell it was decimated, none left but a few scattered frightened wretches crouching down among the scanty cover in the creek bed, knowing full well that to show themselves but for a moment was to court death swift and certain. So they avenged Dick Stanesby's hutkeeper.

They count Dick Stanesby a good fellow in his county. He is a just landlord, well beloved by his tenants. He is a magistrate and stanchly upholds law and order; and withal he is a jolly good fellow, whose hunting breakfasts are the envy and admiration of the surrounding squires. His wife is pretty too, somewhat insipid perhaps, but a model wife and mother, and always sweet and amiable.

There have been found men who were Goths enough to object to Mrs. Stanesby's innocent, loving prattle about her eldest boy and her third girl, and the terrible time they had when her second little boy had the measles, and they were so terrified for the first twenty-four hours lest it should turn to scarlet fever; there have been men, I say, who have objected to this as "nursery twaddle," but their womenkind have invariably crushed them. They believe in Mrs. Stanesby and in Dick Stanesby too.

"Their story is too sweet," says Ethel De Lisle, his sister's sister-in-law. "It reminds one that the chivalry of the olden times has not yet died out among true Englishmen. Only think, he loved silently because he was too poor to speak. He went away to Australia, and he worked and waited there all among the blacks and all sorts of low people, and at the end of four years, when his cousin died and left him Heyington, he came back faithful still and he married her. I call it too sweet for words.".

But Mrs. De Lisle has never met Guy Turner. He is still "riding tracks" on Jinfalla, and consequently she knows nothing of Dick Stanesby's hutkeeper, or of a solitary grave by the Woonawidgee creek.

THE YANYILLA STEEPLECHASE

My dear, my dear, so you want to know why I am an old maid?

Well, nobody asked me to marry them, I suppose that must have been it.

No? What? You think I must have been pretty. Pretty, was I pretty?

They said I was then, dear, but you see there wasn't another lady within fifty miles, and that made the difference, just all the difference. You 've a pretty little girl, Hope—it wasn't fair to have called you Hope, it's such an unlucky name—but if you'd been young when I was they'd just have raved about you.

Had I lovers, dear?

Of course I had lovers. Every woman who isn't downright repulsive has, I think. Willie Maclean doesn't come here to see me, does he? Ah! I thought—

There, never mind, there's no harm done. It's thirty years since the men used to ride across the ranges just to stay the night at Yanyilla, and I don't *think* it was wholly for your grandfather's society they came. Of course I had lovers. It's so long ago I can tell you about them now; but mostly, dear, I don't think a woman should tell. She gets the credit of it, I know, but she ought not to, and I do think there are many things a nice woman, I mean a good woman, keeps to herself.

Oh yes! I had lovers, like every other girl, but there was only one I cared about—and I cared—I cared—I believe I care still, for all I lost him three and thirty years ago. I used to look forward to dying and meeting him in heaven, dear, but I was young then, and after I passed thirty, and began to go down hill, I got to know that he'd never recognize in an old woman the girl he loved on earth. It troubled me sorely, sorely, for he was only thirty when he died, but afterwards I thought we must have been put into this weary world for some good purpose, and surely if there is a great God he won't let me waste my life for nothing. I have tried to do my best, but somehow my life has been a failure all round; I 'm not much use to anybody. They say love doesn't last, but I think they are wrong; I know it has lasted me all these years, and the thought of seeing him again—well, well, you will think an old woman foolish, dear, but it makes my heart beat like a young girl's. Suppose—suppose I should not be quite all he thought me; suppose he should have changed.

Why, Hope, you're smiling at my foolishness, but isn't that the way every woman feels when she's in love; and I 'm in love still, after three and thirty years, God help me, and a woman in the main is always the same, whether her hair is golden, or whether it 's grey and she hides it under a cap.

But this isn't telling you my story, is it, child?

Not that there's much to tell. You know Yanyilla. You know what a station was like in the old days. They have been described over and over again. But Yanyilla was always a nice place. A hundred and eighty miles from Melbourne is a good way even now in these railway days, and it was much further when we had to do the whole journey by Cobb's coach. Oh, we were very much out of the world, and at first I used to feel lonely. My father—well you know pretty well what kind of a man your grandfather was, so it's no use my trying to gloss over his character—and your grandmother, ah, my poor mother, I was always fond of my mother, but she had a hard life, and it made her fretful and not much of a companion for a young girl. She thought the world was a hard place for a woman to live in, and the sooner I found it out and indulged in no vain hopes the better for me. I thought then, rather vaguely to be sure, that she was wrong, and I know it now. But she is dead long, long ago, and perhaps she too knows it. Then there was my brother Ben, your father, Hope, he was always a dear good boy, but he was so much younger than me, I don't suppose he ever thoroughly understood it all.

The homestead was just on the slope where the hills ran down into the plain country. Away to the west and north stretched the dull grey plains far as the eye could see, and behind us to the east and south were the ranges; dull and grey too, I used to think when first I went there, but I changed my mind afterwards. When the sun shone he transformed all things, and the sun shone very often in those days—he does so still maybe, if only I could see with the same eyes—and I loved those ranges. I liked to steal away on a hot day into the deep fern gullies, where the tall green tree-ferns were high over my head, and the dainty maidenhair grew among the rocks and stones at my feet. And someone else loved those gullies too—it's all part of the story, dear, the same old story which comes to every woman at least once in her life.

The boundary between Yanyilla and Telowie was among those ranges, and Paul Griffith was the overseer at Telowie. I met him once or twice at musters at our place, and then we met again once or twice by accident in the gullies, where he was looking for stray cattle and I was gathering ferns. It was only once or twice it was by accident, afterwards it was by design. I can't tell you now exactly how we made the appointments without putting it into so many words; but you are a girl, I dare say you will understand thoroughly. Ah! he was so good-looking, my Paul, so tall and fair and strong, and he had such kind blue eyes. Ah dear, ah dear, how different my life might have been!

Well it went on and on all through the months of August and September, and each time we parted the parting grew harder, and each time we met it was—I can't tell you—just heaven to me, I think. Then one day—shall I ever forget it?—he told me that he loved me, but he told me too how poor he was, far too poor to ask my father for me; for though we were very poor ourselves, my mother had a way of always saying that never should her daughter be as badly off as she had been, so he knew and I knew it was hopeless to think of our being engaged. He said he ought not to see me again, and he would go away; but I cried then, I could not help it, the world seemed such a dreary place without him. Then—it was my fault, I suppose it generally is the woman's fault—he took me in his arms and called me his little girl, and kissed me again and again. He ought not to have kissed me if we were to part, he ought not. You know the old couplet:

"Take hands and part with laughter,

Touch lips and part with tears."

And so it was with us, but it was not his fault I loved him, I loved him with all my heart, and I wanted to be kissed, and those kisses have cost me—no matter what they have cost me—I know now they were worth it.

But we could not make up our minds to part I was young and so was he, and first I made him tell me he loved me better than anything on earth, and then I laughed and said if it was only his poverty that stood between us, I would wait for him all my life. I wondered afterwards at my boldness—it did seem terribly bold, but there was nothing else to be done—it seemed the only thing, I believe it was the only thing, as I should have found it so utterly impossible to take my mother into my confidence, and so you see, my dear, we two embarked on that most foolish of all things, a secret engagement. But the fault was not his, it was mine entirely. He wanted to go and tell my father all about it; it would be better, he said, to be open and above board, and he didn't think my father would mind much; but I wouldn't let him.

I can excuse myself even now, for I was young, and I felt I could not stand my mother's perpetual moan. She would have spoiled my Eden with her prognostications of possible evil. We met in the nearest gully whenever we had the chance, and after all it was not so bad. Now I look back on those two months of spring as the very happiest of my life. If anything went wrong at home, and things did go wrong very often, for my father was sure to be drunk once a week, and my mother's misery made me unhappy, I always consoled myself with the reflection that Paul would understand, that Paul would pity and comfort me. And he never failed me, not once, my darling, not once.

Then there came upon me a new and unexpected trouble, one I might have foreseen had I been a little older and known something more of the world's ways. Stanton of Telowie owned all the country for miles back, and consequently was a well-to-do man. I do not think he was a very reputable man, though he was my father's great friend and boon companion. My mother, usually so hard on men who drank ever so little, and, as she said, led my father astray, would never blame Dick Stanton. It was for my sake he did it, she said, and I don't know now whether she was right or not; he sold out and went to England thirty years ago, and I have never heard of him since. But I do know Paul Griffith, his overseer, hated him with a bitter hatred, and what Paul did I did. I was not a bad-looking little girl, and he may probably have meant to be kind, but it was not his kindness I wanted. Like many another man in those days, he wanted a wife, and this my mother dinned into my unwilling ears morning, noon, and night.

"But, mother," I said at last, driven to bay, "how do you know he wants me?"

"My dear," she answered, "do you think I have lived all these years in the world for nothing? What do you suppose the man comes here twice a week for?"

"To see father," I answered hotly, "and I hate him for it. Why can't he let us alone? He comes, and it's always 'Another bottle, Hope; open another bottle for Mr. Stanton.' I hate him, mother, I hate him."

"Oh, Hope," she went on unheeding, "it would be such a great thing for you. He's worth at least three thousand a year, and he's head over heels in love with you. Think what it'd be, child, never to be worried about money again," and she sighed; my poor mother, she had been worried about every conceivable thing, and more especially this weary money, all her life, and she never expected to be free from care again.

"Think what it 'd be like to be tied to a brute like Dick Stanton all your life!" But she only shook her head and said again, "he was so much in love with me I could do what I liked with him;" and then she added, that if I did not know what was good for me, she, my mother, did, and she would take care my interests did not suffer. It was her duty to look after them as my mother, and she would. Oh! that little word "duty"! It seems to me all sorts of petty cruelties are committed in the name of "duty." And after that Dick Stanton never came to the house, but I, more unwilling than ever, was sent for to entertain him. Even now I don't know whether he really cared, or whether it was simply that he wanted a wife, and I was the only decent-looking girl within reach. And I hated him for it with all my heart, and at last, as things got worse, for my mother had told him that my coldness was all shyness on my part, I was so miserable and perplexed I cried my heart out in the gully, and Paul came and found me and got the whole truth out of me. How angry he was! I can see him now walking up and down talking to himself, and I dried my eyes and began to think things were not half so bad, since I had thrown all my cares on him.

"But Paul," I said, with an attempt at a smile, "you know after all it's very foolish of me to make such a fuss. They can't make me marry a man I don't want to. And I hate him, I hate him. You just don't know how I hate him."

"My darling," he said, sitting down on a log and drawing me towards him, "how am I to help you? I can't have my little sweetheart's life worried out of her in this way. Hope, I had better go to your father and tell him all about it."

"And that would end it all effectually," I sobbed. "Mother would say I was too young to know my own mind. She would say once you were away I would forget you, and she would get Dick Stanton to—to—"

"Give me the sack," said Paul bitterly. "Who knows; perhaps it might be best for you. I 'm not bringing you much happiness, dear."

"Yes, yes, yes; what should I do without you, Paul? I wish I had not told you! You know—you must know—you're all the happiness I have in my life."

"I 'm sure," he said, kissing me fondly, "you make all the brightness in mine. But what am I to do to help you?"

"Just nothing. As I said before, they must give me a say in the matter before they marry me right out."

"My colonial oath! Here 's a nice deceitful piece of baggage! Upon my word, Miss Hope! So you 're the shy little girl who's quite overcome if a fellow so much as looks at her!"

He was standing on the rise of the hill close above us, and how he had come there without our seeing I 'm sure I don't know, except that lovers always are caught sooner or later, and I suppose it was our fate. I 'd rather almost anybody than Dick Stanton had caught us though; for he was a vindictive little wretch, I always felt, and whether he cared for me or not he would not like to find himself cut out by his own overseer. We two sprang apart guiltily, and I saw my lover's face grow red and angry, but not as dark and threatening as the one above me.

"So Mr. Griffith," said our unwelcome third party, "it's you who 've been poaching on my manor. What the devil do you mean by it, sir?"

Paul, I saw, was too angry to trust himself to speak, only he waved his hand to me as if he would have sent me home; but I was too frightened to go. I was not twenty remember, and it seemed to me the two men were on the brink of a violent quarrel, and vaguely I hoped my presence might restrain them. I was wrong, I know now; I ought to have gone, and perhaps—who can tell? But there—all the misery of our lives is just summed up in thinking whether we might not have acted differently. And so I took no notice of Paul, though I saw he wanted me gone, and I stayed. Then Dick Stanton, seeing Paul did not speak, for the moment lost all control of himself, and raged and stormed and used such language as I had never heard in my life before, and I was well accustomed to bad language; for my father, when he had pretty well got to the bottom of the brandy bottle, didn't care much what he said, but he never spoke as Dick Stanton did; oh, never. He was a gentleman at least, my father. Paul stood it just for a minute; I think he was too dumb-founded to speak, and then he made one step forward and caught the other man by the neck—he was so tall and strong, my sweetheart—and shook him as if he had been a child. It was Dick Stanton's turn to look surprised then, and at first he swore harder than ever; then all at once he looked up in Paul's face and burst out laughing.

"What the devil are we quarrelling about, Griffith?" he said, and his voice sounded amiable, though I never would have trusted him.

Paul was still very angry, and only made some unintelligible reply, and Stanton went on with a smile which I thought rather forced.

"I say, Griffith, old chap, you needn't cut up so blessed rough. It's me who ought to cry out, I think. I go courting a girl; I've made that plain enough in all conscience. All the country round knows it, and her father and mother go dinning it into me that she 's awful fond of me, but she 's young and she 's shy—oh so shy!—and the first time I come across the ranges I find this— this—"

I really think he was too angry to think of a word to call me, for he skipped out my name altogether, and went on, "and there I find her cuddled up in your arms."

"She has a right to choose," said Paul, a little sullenly.

"And she has chosen. Just my blooming luck all over."

"And seeing she has chosen," said Paul, still angry, "suppose you leave me to see her safe home."

"And what'll papa say, Miss Hope? He'd rather have the rich squatter for a son-in-law than a poor roustabout, I 'll bet."

"It's no business of my father's," I said hotly, and then he laughed sneeringly.

"By Jove! Dan Forde 'll have something to say to that, or I 'm very much mistaken. Just you wait till to-night," and he turned away and ran up the hill to where, I suppose, he had left his horse. Some one must have told him to come and look for us, of course; he 'd never have come to that lonely gully, and on foot, too, else; but to this day I don't know who it was.

Paul comforted me all he knew; but still I went home very frightened, though I wouldn't let him come with me. I did not quite believe Dick Stanton would be quite so mean as to carry out his threat and tell my father, and if he did not, I was glad, now that it was all over, that he should understand how unwelcome were his attentions to me.

That night he came round as usual, and as usual I was sent for to pour out their brandy for them, and to make myself pleasant to the guest. He did not say anything to make me feel uncomfortable, indeed he was almost kind and I had never liked him better, only I saw in his eyes he had not forgotten the meeting of the morning and did not mean that I should either. Presently they began to talk about the race meeting. We always had a race meeting at Yanyilla once a year, just about the beginning of November. I forget whether there was a cup in those days, but I know all the people about were quite as much excited about the Yanyilla meeting as you are now about the cup. The township was on our run, only three miles away, and took its name from the station, and the paddock we used as a race course was just within sight of the house. We always took great interest in the races, more especially those for the station horses, which were all supposed to be grass-fed, and therefore, when my father and his friend got on the subject of the entries, I felt quite safe and breathed quite freely for the first time that evening.

"I 've entered Boatman for the Yanyilla Steeplechase," said my father, "but I 'm blest if I know who I 'll get to ride him. The beggar's an awful powerful brute, and all the boys are afraid."

"And grass-fed! Surely not. He can't do much harm."

"Oh, he 's a brute, I must confess," said my father, "and no mistake; but he's all there, and if I can get anybody to risk it, I 'll put the pot on him."

"You think he's good to win, then? Can he beat my Vixen?"

"Beat her! He 'll beat any horse this side of the Dividing Range, once he gets started with the right man on his back. But there's just the difficulty."

"Now, I 'll find you a man to ride. He thoroughly understands horses, I 'll say that for him, though I have no cause to love him. He 'll ride for you, but I don't believe Boatman is as good as Vixen."

"I 'll lay you anything you like he is, if only I get the right man up."

"Done with you, then. You shall have the right man, that I promise. Mind, you said anything I liked. You won't go back on your word?"

"Anything to within half my kingdom," laughed my father, who was getting a good way down his bottle, or I 'm sure he never would have agreed to what Dick Stanton asked.

"That's settled, then, for I suppose you don't count your daughter near half your kingdom," said Stanton, and he looked at me as if he would have said, "See how I pay you out. Then if Vixen beats Boatman I marry your daughter out of hand; that's the arrangement, isn't it?"

To this day, in spite of after events, I don't believe he was in earnest, for no man could seriously want to marry a girl who had just shown him as plainly as possible she was in love with another man. I think he just wanted to torment and frighten me by showing me his power, as part punishment for my behaviour of the morning. But I didn't think so at the time. For the moment astonishment took my breath away, and then, when I found my voice, I vehemently protested.

"No! no!" I cried, "I will never marry you! Never! never! I hate you! If you only knew how I Hate you!"

And the two men only laughed at me. My father was more than half through his bottle, or he would never have shamed me so, but the other man was sober enough, he knew what he was doing, and I think was pleased to move me, for usually I would not look at him. I think sometimes now it was the sight of my helpless anger made him carry the joke so far.

"Well, well, you shall have her if you're first past the post," said my father, leaning back in his chair, and laughing heartily, "but I 'm thinking there 'll be two Vixens over at Telowie then, and I know which I 'd rather have the riding of."

"Oh! trust me. Gently does it. Ride her with the snaffle, with just a touch of the spur now and then, just to show her you mean business," and he looked me full in the face and laughed, as if he were taunting me with my helplessness.

If I shut my eyes I can see them now, for all it is so long ago. The long, low, poorly-furnished room, badly lighted by one colza oil lamp, the head of a dingo and two brushes crossed, over the mantelpiece, the only attempt at ornament, and the two men seated at the table, the decanter between them, gambling away my life and happiness. Maybe it was only in jest; I try to think so now, but the consequences were so fatal, there must have been just a spice of earnest in it even then, at least on Dick Stanton's part. But not on my father's. Even now I pray that my father was not in earnest.

The more I protested, the more determined they grew, till at last my mother came in to see what all the laughter was about, and promptly sent me to bed, and the last thing I heard as I made my escape through the door was Dick Stanton's mocking voice calling, "Well, we needn't fear but there'll be plenty of entries for the Yanyilla Steeplechase, once the boys get to hear that Miss Hope Forde is to be the prize."

My mother followed me to my room. I think she, too, was a little angry, but she wouldn't allow it to me, she only scolded me for stopping in the parlour so long.

"You ought to know better at your age," she said. "It was wrong and foolish of you to stop when you saw they were getting excited." My mother always glossed a disagreeable truth over to herself in that way. She never said, "Your father has had too much to drink," though he had at least once a week, but it was always, "Your father is excited," or "over-tired." My poor mother; I have learned to pity her for those deceptions that deceived nobody, since I have grown older and wiser. Still, that night she was hard on me. Perhaps because she felt I had been hardly dealt with, and she had nobody else to vent her anger on. That is the way with some people.

"Don't be silly, now, and cry," she said, for I had flung myself down on my little bed, and was vainly trying to suppress the sobs that would come, "It's not the least good in the world to cry. You shouldn't have stopped so long. It's entirely your own fault. You have nobody to blame but yourself. There, there, for heaven's sake, child, don't cry like that, they 'll have forgotten all about it to-morrow morning, when their heads are clear. I don't know what was the matter with Dick Stanton, I never saw him so excited."

I could have told her, but I held my peace, and she went away, and I cried myself to sleep.

But the matter was not forgotten next day, for my father told us, as if it were a huge joke, that he had bet me against a hundred pounds that Boatman could win the grass-fed steeplechase.

"So you see," he said, laughing at the recollection, "it cuts both ways. If I lose I get my daughter comfortably settled in life, and if I win I 'm at least 100L. to the good."

I looked at my mother appealingly, but she only shook her head. My father was not a man whose whims could be lightly crossed, and she would not let me even try. Ashamed! oh, child! I was never so ashamed in my life! I hung my head all day and was afraid even to look the servant maid in the face. I felt she must despise a girl whose own father held her so lightly, And Paul, there 's where the hardest part of all came. How was I to tell my lover what my father had done? And how was I not to tell him, for I knew that Dick Stanton was not the man to keep such a wager to himself; he would bruit it abroad, if it were only for the sake of angering his rival. I was ashamed, ashamed, ashamed. It seemed to me I could never hold up my head again, and oh, how was I to meet Paul! I thought of nothing else for the next two days, and I had not a chance of seeing him or telling him, for posts were not in those days. And so, though he was only ten miles away, I had to wait two whole days before I saw him again. Then we met in the gully under the shade of the tree ferns. I remember now how the sunlight, coming through their great fronds, made a pattern as of dainty lace work on my white dress, and I studied that pattern carefully, and tried to make out what it reminded me of, though I heard quite plainly a man crushing through the bracken. That is just like a woman though, she longs and longs, and when at last the longed-for hour has come, she is frightened at her own temerity, and half wishes herself back again. I was not often afraid to meet Paul, but I was to-day, and I never looked up till I felt his arm around me and his dear voice in my ear.

"Why, my little girl, my little girl, what is the matter with my little girl?"

Then I told him, with my face hidden on his broad shoulder, I told him, and he was very angry. I knew he would be, but I had not realized how angry, and I was fairly frightened.

"Oh, Paul!" I could only gasp, "Oh, Paul!"

He swore an oath when he saw that I was trembling, and recovered himself a little. Just occasionally, I think, a woman likes the man she loves to be thoroughly angry, and if he does swear then she accepts it as a relief to her own feelings as well as his. So I did not mind Paul swearing, seeing that he was not given to that sort of thing. I felt he was entirely in sympathy with me, and was glad of it.

"What a fool I have been," he said, "what an utter fool. I might have known there was something up when Stanton came to me so confoundedly civil all at once. He made me a sort of apology for his rudeness to you the other day, congratulated me on my good luck in winning you, and then finally suggested that I should ingratiate myself with your father by offering to ride Boatman for him in the grass-fed steeplechase, and of course—"

"You said 'No!' Oh, Paul! you said 'No!'"

"No! darling, of course I said 'Yse.' What else could I say? And I wanted to please your father. How could I know—that—that—what the fellow was up to."

"But now, Paul, you won't ride him, now you do know, will you, my dearest?" And because I was afraid he would, I put my arms coaxingly round his neck and tried to draw his face down to mine. It did not want much trying, he was always ready enough to kiss me, my dear love, but he shook his head when I tried to dissuade him from riding Boatman.

"After all, sweetheart," he said, "I really think I'm the proper person to ride the grey. If you're to be the prize, well it can't make any more talk, my riding, and, of course, it will give me a sort of right to you."

"But—but—you mustn't ride Boatman, you mustn't—you mustn't—you mustn't. He baulks, and he runs down his fences, and he pulls, and—and—oh, my darling! you mustn't ride Boatman!"

"What a list of crimes," he said, smiling at my vehemence. "Still, I have ridden a horse or two in my life, and I'm inclined to think I 'm equal to this one. He can beat anything, your father tells me, this side of the Dividing Range. I had a trial this morning, and I 'm inclined to think the old gentleman hasn't put too high a value on him. Boatman's an out-and-outer, once one gets on good terms with him. And there 's the difficulty no one can manage him."

I knew then it was little good my speaking; dearly as he loved me, nay, for my sake even, he was determined to ride Boatman. And after all, looked at from his point of view, I think he was right.

Stanton's Vixen was the only horse in the running, the only one in the least likely to win, and if I was to be the prize, as my father insisted, not once but twenty times, then, indeed, it was very necessary that our horse should be well ridden, and I knew, and he knew, nobody could do that so well as Paul. Then I don't know what dark presentiments filled my mind, but something told me he should not ride in that race, something told me all was not fair and above board, and with all my strength, with all my powers of persuasion, I tried to stop him. I coaxed him, and he only stroked my hair fondly, told me I had nice dark eyes and pretty hair, and said if I made myself so sweet and dear, it only showed him all the more clearly I must be won by fair means or foul. Are you smiling, Hope? Ah, my dear, it is three-and-thirty years ago, and the remembrance of days like those is all I have. Then I stormed and raged, every unkind term I could think of I heaped on him, and that is like a woman too, I think—when all other means fail she tries anger.

Did he think, I asked, I was so slight a thing as to be bought and sold in that manner? Did he think that my father could give me away in that way, as if I were a horse or a bullock; and then, of course, just as I would have given anything to be dignified and grand, I spoiled it all, for my voice failed, and I burst into tears.

He was good to me! oh, he was good to me! He would not give up his point, but he comforted me, and he was good. Once I had fairly started I could not stop; all the pent-up misery of the last three days seemed bound up in those tears. Heaven knows never had woman greater cause for tears, though I only dimly felt it then, and never since have I cried as I cried that day. Paul was frightened at first, I think, for he said nothing but, "Poor little girl, poor little girl," and held me closer than ever, but he would not give in, and at last, tired out, I could only sob.

"Must you ride him, Paul, must you ride him?"

"I must, my darling. I really think it is the only thing to be done, both for your sake and my own. It was a brutal thing to do, but it was none of my doing, and when Boatman passes the winning post with Paul Griffith up, why that settles everything, doesn't it, my sweet?"

Ah, yes, that would have settled everything; and as he stood there beside me, so tall and straight and strong, I made up my mind my tears were idle tears, and it would all come right in the end. And before I went home we were both more than half convinced that there was likely to be more good in my father's foolish wager than at first sight appeared, and we two would turn it to our own advantage. Paul, indeed, was jubilant, once he had got over his anger. He had come to tell me he had got the offer of the managership of a station across the border in Riverina. He would take it at the end of the year; there was a house a lady could live in—and—well—would I go? After he had won—fairly won—the Yanyilla Steeplechase, should he go to my father and ask for the wife he had won?

And he was so confident, so happy, so certain of success, how could I fail to be happy and confident too? I went home that night with a far lighter heart than I had carried for many a long day. My mother saw the traces of tears, and asked what I had been crying for, but I kept my own counsel, for where was the good of enlightening her till I could tell her everything was settled? There are many in the world who can rejoice with them that rejoice, many, quite as many, thank God for it, who will weep with them that weep; but to very few is it given, I think, to share another's anxiety sympathetically. Fear and hope, we hardly know which predominates, and the pain, which is of necessity the result, is best borne in silence and alone. And at first with me hope reigned supreme; but not for long though.

One morning, a few days after Paul and I had settled matters so very much to our own satisfaction, the boy who brought up the milkers fell sick, and Ben, who took his place, failed to find them. It was a thing of not infrequent occurrence, and I turned out as usual to help him. As usual, too, those wretched cows had turned up the creek and lost themselves in the gullies among the ranges to the south. As the grass grew dry-on the plains they would wander along the sheltered creek, where in patches it was still fresh and green. And this day they had wandered farther than usual. We rode on and on, our horses stumbling among the rough ground, till at last we heard the cracked old cow bell and knew they were found.

"Coming towards us too," said Ben. "I wonder what started 'em."

"They knew it was time to come home," I suggested; but Ben wouldn't agree with me, and he knew a good deal about cattle for a boy of his age. Then we turned a shoulder of the hill, and there were the four wanderers making straight for us. There was something else besides, a tent pitched on a nice green patch of grass, and a horse feeding out of a bucket close beside it. A man at the door snatched up the bucket as we appeared and carried it into the tent, but I saw it as clearly as I see you now, and if I could not trust my own eyes there was Ben, and he saw it too.

He was quicker than I too, for he had been about among the men and heard them talk about such things.

"O my!" he said. "Here's a go! That's Vixen, Stanton's mare. She's a regular take down, ain't she? She looks like an awful old stock horse, don't she? Look here, Sissy, I believe they 're feeding her on the sly. What was she drinking out of that bucket?"

We turned the cows homewards, and then went towards the little tent. It was Vixen sure enough, and Stanton's man, Dan O'Connor—Ticket-of-leave Dan, as they called him—was in charge. He bid us "Good morning" in the oily, slimy tones of the old convict, and said he was just going to bring back our stray cows.

"I seed the Yanyilla brand on 'em, and I guessed some one 'd be around lookin' for 'em soon, as they was milkers," he said, and what could I say.

We and our cattle were the trespassers, for this bit of country belonged to Telowie, and Dick Stanton was only doing as others did when he sent out his horse to a picked bit of sweet grass in order to fit her for the coming race. She might have been drinking water out of the bucket. I had no possible means of knowing that she had not, and yet I felt sure, with Ben, that there had been oatmeal in the bucket, and that Vixen, who, until it had got about that Paul Griffith was to ride Boatman, had been first favourite for the Yanyilla Steeplechase, was being fed. I rode right up to the tent in order to be quite sure, and saw on the grass where the bucket had stood, a few white grains as of oatmeal, and Ben, whose eyes were keener for that sort of thing, saw them too. But what could we do? It was quite the thing for the horses that were going to run in the grass-fed steeplechase to be carefully fed by their owners or backers on some place where the grass seemed fresher, greener, and sweeter than anywhere else. About twenty horsts were entered, and all along the banks of the Yanyilla and Telowie Creeks, just before the race meeting, you might come across camps such as Ben and I had struck this morning. Boatman himself was camped not a mile from the house by the big water-hole, and thither went my father and Paul every day to see that he was getting on all right. Even now I don't understand my father's conduct; you 'd think no sensible man would have seriously considered the foolish wager he had made, and yet I had a feeling that he cared very little about his own horse's chances and a great deal about Vixen's. He used to laugh to Paul and say, "He's good enough; he's good enough." But in the evening, after a glass or two of Battle-axe brandy, my mother and I heard quite a different story. Boatman's chances grew very small, and Boatman's vices were so magnified that I could not sleep for fear. And when I told my sweetheart he only laughed, and said he knew the old horse now a good deal better than his master, and though he was a bad-tempered old brute there was not a horse in the colony could touch him, once you took him the right way. It was like a woman to be so full of fears and forebodings, and this morning, now that I seemed to have good ground for them, my fears redoubled, and Ben and I, in our excitement, fairly raced those milkers home, for which my mother very properly scolded me well. That troubled me little enough. I was all anxiety to see Paul, and waited down at the little camp watching Boatman crop the grass till he paid his daily visit, and then I poured into his ears all my fears. And Hope—he only laughed, turned up my face and kissed me, and laughed at my discovery and my fears.

"So that 's his little game, is it?" he said. "Well, I always knew he was a pretty bad lot, but I hardly thought he'd descend to that. Let him feed her. The little corn they dare smuggle into the mare won't make any difference in the end. So cheer up, my little girl. Only a week more now and then we 'll see."

That week, that week, my last week of happiness, and to think I wished it over! Oh! Hope, Hope! never wish the time gone child! you may be wishing away the last happy days of your life, as I did!

Every day now I saw Paul, every day we met at the camp where was Boatman, and after seeing he was all right wandered away into the gullies together. I could not help being anxious, very anxious, and as the time grew nearer it grew worse to bear; but still it was a happy time with Paul by my side, with his strong arm to lean on, with his kind face so near to my own. I wonder why one's happy days in this world are so brief. It has often seemed to me the arrangements of Providence are a little hard.

We always managed to have three days' racing at Yanyilla, and all the country side for miles round gave itself up to the delights of racing; and of course that meant a week's dissipation, just like "cup week" in Melbourne now. The last day was always an off-day—an afterthought—not arranged for in the original programme; I don't know exactly for what reason they held it, except that they thought it a pity not to make out the week. I fancy the races on the last day were very poor affairs, only got up because the men had got the racing fever on them, and wanted to bet on something; but I ought not to say much, for I really don't know. My interest in racing came to an end for ever that first day, and I have never seen a race run since, and never shall in this world. I don't suppose they ever have races in the next.

The eventful day came at last, the first Tuesday in November, the day that would be "cup day" now-a-days. Monday was an exciting day for us. The stewards came out and saw to the preparing of the racecourse, which was ordinarily simply a piece of flat paddock close to Yanyilla homestead, and it seemed the entire population of the township accompanied them, to see that it was properly done, I suppose, and not only the entire population of the township, but of all the district round I think. My father was in his glory. He was a most hospitable man, and everyone he came across he asked up to the house, regardless of the fact that we were already as full as we could possibly be, and that long before mid-day my mother and I were weary washing and rewashing our very limited stock of glasses, for the visitors who came, if they did nothing else, partook very freely of our brandy. That is the way with many good-natured people, I think; my father was voted a jolly good fellow by his guests, and I don't suppose anybody ever thought that the hardest part of the work fell on us two women. I ought not to complain now, it is all over so long ago, but I have always felt it a terribly hard thing that the last happy day I had should have been so utterly spoilt. Paul and I had arranged to spend it together down in the gully where we first made each others acquaintance; he had come to the house for me; he had grown bolder now that he was to ride my father's horse, and there he sat on the verandah, waiting more than half the day, while I washed and wiped that seemingly endless array of glasses.

Do you wonder that I complain, Hope?

Even now, if I shut my eyes, I seem to see the glorious November sunshine beckoning me out, to hear the impatient shuffle of my lover's feet as he sat and waited, and yet there seemed no prospect of release for me. At last, I suppose my mother guessed something of my feelings, for when the kitchen clock was on the stroke of four she said—

"You can go now, Hope. If they want any more they 'll just have to drink it out of dirty glasses," and I went gladly, and selfishly too, for I knew whatever she might say, I had left her to bear the burden and heat of the day alone. Still I am glad—even now I am deeply thankful to my mother—for those hours of happiness she gave me, almost, I think, unconsciously.

Down in the gully Paul and I watched the shadows grow longer as the day crept on towards evening, and I tried once more to dissuade him from riding Boatman. I might just as well have spoken to the winds.

"My dear child," he said a little severely, "you must know you are asking an impossibility. All the district round has put its money on the horse because I 'm riding, and they say I 'm the only man in the district that can ride him. I never could play it so low down on your father as to desert him at the last moment. Don't you see, my darling?"

I didn't see. But what was I to do? I saw he was still a little weak from the effects of an attack of fever and ague he had had some time before, but when I urged that as a reason he only laughed, and said I was a very Job to worry myself about such trifles; as for the fever there was hardly a trace of it left, and it was tact, not strength, Boatman wanted to ride him. Then there was nothing more to be said. I could only put my arms round his neck and tell him it was only my love for him made me foolishly anxious, and he must not think badly of me for it. After all, it was only natural I should be anxious; he would have had more cause to grumble if I had not been.

I got little enough sleep that night. Early in the evening my father and the most of his guests went down to the principal public-house in the township to look at the general entries—why I 'm sure I don't know, for they must have known well enough for weeks beforehand what horses were going to run—and then late at night they, or rather my father and one or two choice spirits, came home, and through the thin partition I could hear them talking and shouting, and drinking interminable healths, and when I heard them drink the health of "the Prize for the Yanyilla Steeplechase," I covered my face with the clothes and tried to hear no more, for I knew by the shout of laughter that accompanied the toast that they were thinking of my father's foolish wager. The summer dawn crept in through the windows before they reeled off to bed, and I, wearied and tired, realised that at last the day I dreaded so was here, and a few more hours would put me out of my misery.

That is what Paul said when he met me on the verandah soon after breakfast, for he had stayed the night in the township, so as to be close at hand, and the smile I gave him in return was very near to tears. I think he saw that, for he hastily directed my attention to the crowd of people already assembled, and laughed, and said there was no fear but Yanyilla Races would be a success this year.

They were content with very primitive arrangements in those days, my dear. How the secretary of the least flourishing turf club in Victoria nowadays would stare if he could see the humble shed where the riders weighed out, and the still more humble judge's box made of boughs, a bad imitation of a blackfellow's mia-mia. And more primitive even than the judge's box was the refreshment booth, where the landlord of the *Bushman s Rest* dispensed drinks to all who could afford to pay for them, or could get others to do so in their stead. The racehorses, I remember, were merely hitched up to a post and rail fence in the most ordinary fashion. But the people—there were all sorts and conditions of men there, and a small sprinkling of women folk, for women were scarce in those days.

As the sun rose higher the crowd grew thicker, till I think there must have been fully fifteen hundred or two thousand people there. Deadman's Creek, the goldfield nearest us, was in full swing, and it seemed to me the place must be deserted that day, for though it was thirty miles away as the crow flies, nobody had thought much of that distance in glorious weather like this. Some of the red-shirted diggers were fine-looking fellows enough; indeed, they ought to have been, for in those days the finest gentleman was not ashamed to try his luck with the pick and shovel like the labouring man who was his neighbour. If he got an honest labouring man he was lucky, for, my dear, the times were rough, and they did say there were a lot of old hands from Tasmania and the Sydney side on Deadman's in those days, and their room would have been better than their company. But those things didn't concern me much. All I thought of was Paul. He stayed with me all the morning, taking me round, showing me how fit and well Boatman looked, pointing out to me the bookmakers already at work, and the men with the three-card trick, and various other devices for passing away the time, and getting at the money of the unwary. Some unfortunate had already got himself into trouble, for what I know not, but I suspected it was too close an acquaintance with the wine when it is red, for over on the other side of the paddock from the house I saw an unfortunate chained to a tree with a stout bullock chain, yelling with all his might, a solemn warning to others not to go and do likewise. The police in the old days were often obliged to make use of such primitive methods of detaining their prisoners—there was no help for it, and nobody minded, not even the unlucky prisoner himself. I suppose he looked upon it as all in the day's work or pleasure, if you will. I tried to take an interest in everything for Paul's sake, but I couldn't.

What did it matter to me how the day went off? What if the howling bookmakers did win the district money? What if it was rumoured that Ben Shepherd's mare was a little off, and not in her usual form, and she was first favourite for the "Telowie Handicap?" It didn't matter to me, nothing mattered to me, if only Boatman was first past the post, and his rider safe and sound at my side again. No, no, what did I care whether he came in first or last? It would make no difference to me, in spite of my father's wager; I wanted the race over, and then, whether Boatman were first or last, Boatman's rider was my sweetheart in the face of all the world, no matter what my father or Dick Stanton should say. Dick Stanton was there, a regular bush dandy, for he was going to ride his own horse, but I would not look at him, though he came over and wished me "Good morning" as if we were the best of friends, and I hated him for it, and I know now my hatred was well founded, for if it had not been for him, I should have been a happy woman this day.

How slowly the morning wore on. It seemed to me it must be somewhere about five o'clock, when there was a stir and a bustle, and the clock struck twelve, and they were preparing for the "Telowie Handicap." I know nothing whatever about that race, though I watched it from the best vantage point on the course, our own verandah. My eyes were too dim to see it, though I heard quite plainly the hoarse roar of the people as the favourite passed the post just a length ahead, and I knew that Paul by my side was shouting with the rest. I was thinking all the time that the next race I should be standing there alone, while my lover was riding the worst-tempered, most unmanageable brute in the colony.

Then, when the race was over, Paul turned to me with a smile, and I felt that the morning, instead of crawling, had taken to itself wings.

"I must go now, dear," he said, and I put my hand on his arm, and without a word drew him into the house, empty now, for everybody was too interested in the racing to stay inside.

"Oh, Paul! Paul! I do try to be brave, but do be careful. For my sake, do be careful."

Perhaps if I had begged of him then, he might have given up the thought of riding. I reproach myself sometimes with not having asked him, but after all, I don't think it would have been any good, only it is the bitterest thing in the world to think "it might have been."

He was so good to me, so good. No one has been so good to me since. He stroked my hair, and kissed me, and comforted me.

"I am a brute," he said, "to bring the tears into those pretty brown eyes."

And I brushed away the tears and tried to tell him again how dear he was to me. But what is the good of going over the old story once again, child. It is just the same old story for every man and woman, with variations so slight as hardly to be worth counting. And yet it is natural that every woman thinks her own love story the most interesting on the face of the earth. No one was ever like her lover, no one was ever loved like she was. I think it is well it should be so. If it is only a fancy, it is a pretty fancy, and the world, or rather the women in it, are much happier for it. I don't know whether it's the same with men. All the years I have lived I don't understand what a man thinks; I don't suppose any woman ever does.

"I shall see a bright face watching for me when I pass the post. Not half an hour now, sweetheart," he said, as he gave me a last kiss, and again he paused on the verandah to wave his hand and to tell me once more not to be afraid.

They were shouting for him as he ran across to the corner that did duty as saddling paddock, and I watched his bright red shirt anxiously. I could keep my eye on him though I found it impossible to see anybody else. My mother called me to attend to something—to lay the cloth for lunch, I think it was— but one glance at my face showed her I was useless.

"Go, child, go," she said, not unkindly, "I 've been afraid of your making a fool of yourself over that man. He's not worth it, as you 'll have found out for yourself before the year is out. Now go and see the race; I'll lay the table."

I went quietly back on to the verandah, and watched the riders being weighed, and the weights being adjusted to the saddles; very primitive were the weights in those days. I saw them wrap up an iron bar in a blanket and strap it on to Boatman's saddle, for though Paul was a fairly heavy man the horse was still more heavily weighted, and then I watched the fifteen horses as they came out and paraded before the assembled crowd. How plainly it seemed to me Paul Griffith stood out from the rest, with the big iron-grey horse. He waved his hand to me as he passed, as one who would say, "There now, you see, there's nothing to be afraid of," and almost for the moment I felt I had exaggerated my fears. I waved my hand in return and watched them as they passed on to the starting post. And then before they got there, there was trouble. The big grey horse, even though he was on the outside, apparently objected to the presence of his kind, and I saw him fallen behind and making desperate efforts to get his head between his forelegs. He kept them all waiting at the post, and the starter called several times; but it was all to no purpose, Boatman was determined to have his own way, and it was fully a quarter of an hour before, very sulkily—for a horse can be sulky—he condescended to walk slowly up to the others. It seemed to give me confidence, that brief respite. Paul was so much master of the situation, in spite of the contrariness of the beast he rode, that I was at once convinced of the foolishness of my fears, and for a moment I felt quite content and free from care as the horses got in line.

It was the race of the day, and there was a hush for an instant, then down went the starter s flag, there was a roar, and a shout from the crowd, "They 're off," and I saw the line of horses stretch themselves out across the plain. The big grey was on the inside striding along about three quarters of a length clear of the others, and just behind came a front rank—so to speak—of half-a-dozen horses, and among them gleamed the dazzling black and yellow stripes of our chief opponent, Vixen. They raced for that first fence at a tremendous pace, and I would have shut my eyes had I not had so much at stake, for the fences were stiff as they are now, and the horses were only grass-fed. But I looked on with a sickening fear at my heart and I saw that Boatman had not forgotten his old trick—right across the line of horses he swerved, and for a moment they were all in confusion, for he collided with two just as they were taking off, and there was a cry of, "He's down, he 's down." "No, no," cried a man alongside me, who was half wild with excitement already, "well picked up, sir; that's the bully boy. Stick to it, old pard, stick to it," and I saw with a beating heart that almost suffocated me, Boatman clear of the ruck, safe on the other side of the fence, and as in a dream I heard the people shouting, "Billy Craig's pony's down, and the Coyote," and I saw two horses wildly careering across the plain,—Billy Craig—I knew him by his green and yellow shirt, made out of his wife's old curtains—pursuing one, while the Coyote's rider had only managed to struggle to his knees, and was slowly rocking himself backwards and forwards with his head in his hands. How could I care for these things; love is so selfish! Only a little while now and the race would be over, and I had no power to think of another's possible pain. All I thought was that the first fence was safely over, and it gave me courage for those that were to come later. One more fence, and then came the jump right in front of the verandah which did duty as a stand, and I held my breath as the horses came up to it in a lump, except the big grey, which was leading by about a length. Quite plainly I saw him, and he was pulling double, but Paul sat like a rock, slightly leaning forward, true bushman as he was, and the old horse jumped beautifully, and got away with a clear lead of about six lengths ahead. I put my arm round the verandah post, for I felt I could hardly stand without support. Speak I could not; all sorts of hopes and fears were madly coursing through my brain, and I listened as a woman beside me put my thoughts into words.

"Oh," she said, with a long-drawn breath, "what an awful pace! And they've got to go round again, too! That horse in front will be done before they've gone much farther."

"Not much," said the man on the other side, scornfully, "that big grey can keep it up for a week. He's all there as long as Griffith can keep him quietly in front. Oh, he's a beautiful jumper, he is, when he's properly ridden, but he's got the devil's own temper. Go it, old pard! go it!" he shouted again, and his enthusiasm gave me such comfort, I would have thanked him had I dared speak.

All around the course I watched them, and at every fence my heart gave a bound of thankfulness as I heard the man beside me shouting hurrahs at Boatman's success. Gladder and gladder I grew, and nothing else in the world mattered to me so long as the big grey was still sailing along, even that he was ahead gave me only a momentary joy, so thankful was I that he was still safe, and likely to be safe.

"He's the best rider that ever I seed, Jim, sure," said the woman beside me, and I could have kissed her for the praise.

"Best rider this side of the Murray," said the man laconically, and Hope, Hope, before me stretched my future, bright, and happy, and smiling, such happiness as I had never dared dream would come into my life. A horse fell, another refused; what was it to me? There was Paul still ahead. Then, at the other side of the course, he was joined by Mick Power's Bangle, and another that I did not recognize, and Vixen's yellow and black stripes went up to within a couple of lengths of the leaders, and a length behind her came the ruck.

"Ah! I told you so," sighed the woman, "they 've collared 'im. Boatman's beat."

"The race's a gift to him," reiterated the man, "if he can only stand up to these three fences. Why, that boy's riding Bangle to keep him in his place already."

A roar went up from the crowd.

"Boatman wins! Boatman! Boatman!"

"Vixen! Vixen!" cried a voice here and there, but they were drowned in a universal cry of, "The grey wins, hands down. Boatman! Boatman!"

I was a happy woman for those brief seconds, the happiest woman in all the wide earth; not a fear for the result troubled me. Already I seemed to feel the glad clasp of Paul's hand, to see the light in his eyes, that would say to me, even though others were present, that he had won his bride, and I watched them coming down to the last fence, the fence that led into the straight, without a tremor.

How could I? How could I? It makes me sick to think of it now, but then I was so certain of success, I put my hand to my throat and took off the little silk handkerchief that I wore there, that I might wave it in triumph, and all round me the people, wild with excitement, were shouting, "Boatman wins! Boatman wins!" It seemed as if they were all in sympathy with me, and in my heart I blessed them for it.

Then, then, oh, Hope! how can I tell you? I didn't understand it for many a long day, and though I saw it with my own eyes, I could not tell you how it happened. All of a sudden the glad shouts of "Boatman wins" changed to one of "They 're down, they're both down," and then, before I had thoroughly grasped the situation, while I still held my little scarf ready to wave, the shout went up just as joyously, oh, just as joyously, "Vixen wins, Vixen! Vixen!"

Even then I did not understand the full extent of my misfortune; other men had fallen and been all right, why not Paul? On my left, the man who had put his money on the grey, swore an oath through his clenched teeth that made me wonder had he as much at stake as I.

What happened? Oh, it was simple enough. They told me afterwards, when it was nothing to me whether a race was ever run again in this world. The grey had the race easily, they said, and was going strong. Paul steadied him for the fence, but in the last couple of strides the Vixen came with a tremendous rush, at the risk of his own neck, they said, and the grey stood off his fence. Such a little thing, dear, such a little thing. Boatman stood off his fence, landed on top, and turned clean over on to his rider. Vixen hit all round, but by rattling good horsemanship—as good as Paul's own, they said—was kept on her legs, and came in winner of the Yanyilla Steeplechase.

I wanted to go to Paul, to rush across to where already a little crowd were collecting. Why should he be hurt—so many had fallen already, and not one was badly hurt—why should he be? No, I told myself, I need not fear, and yet I was afraid to move, and I stood there, and listened to the woman beside me counting the horses as they came in.

"Vixen first, Sandy second, the Dingo—no, Bones third. 'Ard luck on Mr. Griffith, ain't it, Jim? I don't believe the 'orse as got up. Couldn't have killed 'im, eh?"

The whole place was swimming before my eyes, but there came to me a feeling I must know the worst, and I put the little kerchief that was to have waved for my lover's triumph over my head, and started out into the brilliant sunshine towards the little crowd that was collecting round the last fence. The woman tried to stop me.

"Don't 'ee go, dearie, don't 'ee. Jim 'ere'll go," but I pushed her away. Why should she try and stop me, what right had anyone to come between me and my love? Then the crowd parted, and I saw a little procession come towards me. What was that borne by four men? I just caught the gleam of a scarlet jacket, and then some man's voice said, not unkindly:

"It's his sweetheart. For God's sake take her away."

But some one else—the doctor I think—put in a word.

"It can't make any difference. She must know sooner or later, poor child. Lay him down here, under this tree. I doubt if we get him to the house alive."

They laid him under a big blackwood tree, and the doctor put his head on my lap. Such a still white face as it was, with the eyes closed and just a drop or two of blood round the corners of the mouth.

"Oh, doctor," I said, and it seemed to me my own voice was far, far away, farther even than those of the men who were standing around me, "he will get well, he will, he must! He can't be much hurt."

But the doctor said nothing, and the fear that was in my heart grew and grew as I stooped over my lover and, careless of onlookers, kissed him again and again.

"My darling, my darling, my darling, you must get well soon," for I would not see that there was much amiss; ten minutes ago he had been full of life; half an hour ago I had been in his arms.

Very wearily his eyes opened and I saw he knew *me*.

"My poor little girl," he said, "My poor little Hope," and his hand clasped mine as I had dreamed a moment ago it would, as if he would care for me and guard me all through life.

And then—and then—Hope, dear, there isn't any more to tell. He died there in my arms, and at first I could not believe it, but the doctor took me away to my mother, and she was kind to me—yes, she was very tender to me; but what can anyone do when all the happiness has gone out of one's life. Then I began to grow old, dear, though I was not twenty, and I have been growing old ever since.

Why, there 're tears in your eyes, child! Don't cry; I am old now and some of the bitterness has gone. One doesn't understand why the good Lord should let life be so bitter for some of us, but I suppose it is for some good reason, only—only, you see it was another man's wickedness spoiled my life. Yes, yes, I know there was foul play. Dick Stanton rushed his horse down on Boatman like that, just to spoil his chance of the race, and many there were who thought as I did; but who could prove it? No, I don't think even now he meant to kill him.

But there—there is my story, Hope. It is many a long day since I told it. You wanted to know why I am an old maid; you understand now, don't you, dear. I couldn't have married anybody else, how could I? But don't be an old maid, Hope, it is a dreary life—a lonely, hopeless life, and—

Yes, I thought so. Willie Maclean coming up the path. What, blushing, child, or is it my old eyes deceive me? Run away then and bring him in here. I knew his father in the old days, before the Yanyilla Steeplechase was lost and won.

A DIGGER'S CHRISTMAS

It was on the Tinpot Gully diggings, now known to fame by a far more euphonious title, that early in the fifties I spent my first Christmas in Australia. There were all sorts and conditions of men there, men from every nation and every class. Englishmen and Italians, Russians and Portuguese, Persians, Chinamen, and negroes, sons of peers and London pickpockets, all rubbed shoulders on the Tinpot Gully diggings. But they came naturally enough to me in those days. At one and twenty nothing astonishes one, and I took things as I found them, and questioned not, and barely wondered at the mixed company in which I found myself. Very peaceful looked the scene as I stood at my tent door, or rather curtain, and surveyed it thus early in the morning. All the camp was sleeping. Most of the diggers had made a night of it the night before in anticipation of the holiday, and now were sleeping off the effects, so that I had it all to myself, and spite of the havoc wrought by the diggers, the gully was pretty still. We were all camped on the flat that bordered the banks of the creek, and away beyond on all sides stretched the hills, standing out clearly now in the brilliant morning sunlight, range upon range, in a series of blue ridges, till they faded away in the bluer distance. The Union Jack—emblem of authority-floated from the staff in front of the Commissioner's tent, and from my outlook I could see the sunlight gleaming on the carbines of the troopers who stood sentry over the gold tent, and digger as I was, and sworn foe to all troopers, the sunbeams on those carbine barrels gave me a comfortable sense of security, for (for the first time in our diggings' experience) my mate and I had lodged a little chamois leather bag full of gold dust and small nuggets—part of the fortune which we trusted in days to come was to take us back to the old land—with the Commissioner, and I was glad to feel in those wild times that he was fully alive to the nature of his trust. Having satisfied myself as to the safety of my property, I re-entered the tent and roused out my mate.

"Rouse out, Dick, old man! Merry Christmas to you, my boy! Merry Christmas, and many of 'em!"

Dick turned over sleepily, rubbed his eyes, and went through exactly the same performance I had done, before he could rouse himself sufficiently to accompany me across the hills to another creek, where, the bottom being of bed rock, the crystal water was still pure and unsullied by the digger's desecrating hand. Our dip was refreshing; we could only find time for it on Sundays and holidays such as this, and probably we appreciated it all the more for its rarity. Our toilet was simplicity itself. We each arrayed ourselves in a red flannel shirt and moleskin trousers, clean to-day in honour of Christmas, tucked into our high boots, while a slouch hat and a revolver in the belt completed the costume. On our return I proceeded to prepare breakfast, while Dick looked after the sick boy. Breakfast was not sumptuous; all my energies were reserved for dinner, and Dick had to make out as best he might on damper left from the night before, and the cold remains of a nondescript joint of mutton. He came back just as I had got the rough meal ready, reporting poor Wilson as a little better and awfully hungry. Then he tipped the tea—post and rails we used to call it—into our tin pannikins, and proceeded to boil part of a cabbage in the billy for the invalid. I laugh now when I think that in those days we counted a common cabbage a luxury fit to tempt a sick man's appetite; but, indeed, luxuries of all kinds were scarce, and as for that cabbage it had been procured with infinite pains and at great cost; and the odour that rose from the pot—the very offensive odour of boiled cabbage, as I now think it—appeared to us most appetising.

I went with Dick to give poor Bob Wilson his breakfast. It was a very thin, white, pinched face that looked out from among the rough bedclothes, and a skeleton hand that grasped mine.

He appreciated the cabbage, however. I have been told since that it ought to have killed him, but it didn't.

"By Jove!" he said, "it's splendid, splendid. It must have cost a lot to get it. You fellows are good to me. If it hadn't been for you two, I 'd have died like a dog,"—not quite true, for if we hadn't looked after him someone else would—"and before the next year's out I 'll try and show you how grateful I am."

And before the next year was out the poor boy was dead—murdered by some miscreant for the handful of gold in his possession, down in the lonely bush about Reedy Creek.

Wilson's wants being attended to, Dick and I began our preparations for the all important dinner. This was to consist of roast scrub turkey and plum pudding, washed down by Battle axe brandy. And here the good old cookery-book adage came into play, for as yet our bird was running wild in the scrub, and it was a case of first catch your turkey. The morning was hot, but not too hot, with just a pleasant breeze stirring in the bush, and I rather desired to go on the shooting expedition. I ventured to suggest mildly that Dick was a better hand at pudding than I was, but he saw through my little game. Pudding was not an absolute necessary of life, he said, which the turkey really was, and as I was a bad shot—there was no denying the fact, I was a very bad shot—he had better go while I stopped at home and manipulated the pudding.

Dick always had his own way in the end, and I watched him enviously as he tramped up the opposite hill-side until he was lost to view, and then I set to work on the pudding.

The whole camp was astir by now—some busy preparing their morning meal, some like me, beginning on dinner, and many too sick and seedy to think of anything but more brandy, while one or two were good enough to come and favour me with their views on the pudding. We had laid in all the necessaries at least a week before, and then I set to work to stone raisins for the first, and I trust, the last time in my life. It is laborious work. I 'd rather use a pick and shovel any day, but I knew it ought to be done, I had heard my mother say so many a time; so I stuck to it gallantly, and with sticky and aching fingers worked through that pile of raisins. Everything comes to an end at length, and at last I came to the end of those raisins, and poured them into the bucket, where the flour and currants, and sugar and candied peel were already reposing. To these I added a billy of water from the creek, and stirred the lot together with a big stick. My wife informs me that a good plum pudding can't be made without a certain proportion of suet, some spice, and six or seven eggs, but I assure you that was a very excellent pudding, and we never even thought of such things. I don't suppose we could have got them if we had, so it was just as well. After I had mixed my pudding I had one moment of deepest despair. There it lay, a yellow-looking mass at the bottom of the bucket. So far all was well, but how was that yellow mass to be turned into the orthodox jolly-looking plum-pudding? I was cudgelling my brains over this enigma as I lighted up the fire, when one of the admiring crowd round— I suppose he must have, been a past-master in the art of cooking—solved the difficulty for me.

"Ain't you got a pudden-cloth?" he asked.

"By Jingo!" I thought, "of course." But I am thankful to say I did not betray my ignorance.

"A pudding-cloth," I said, as if I had known all about it all along. "No, I haven't a pudding-cloth; I 'm going to use a shirt."

Thereupon I retired to the tent, and procured a red flannel shirt—one of Dick's—which, with the top cut off, answered admirably.

"Don't ye, don't ye now tie it too tight, else it won't 'ave room to swell," implored my self-constituted adviser, and I followed his advice—was only too thankful for it, in fact—and by the time my mate returned with the turkey, the pudding was bubbling away in the bucket which did duty as saucepan as jolly as possible.

Our Christmas dinner was a decided success. The turkey was splendid, and the pudding, bar a slight grittiness, occasioned by my not having washed the currants, which I am told should always be done, was also good, and our guests—we had three besides Bob Wilson (guests who brought their own tin plates and knives and forks)—thoroughly appreciated it.

Nowadays I can't eat wild turkey until it has been hung a certain time, and unless it is served up with gravy, port wine, red currant jelly, and piquante sauce, but then—well, that was an excellent fellow we had for dinner that Christmas Day; I shall never look upon his like again. After dinner, Battle-axe brandy and other drinks, varying only in degrees of strength, being plentiful, the camp became somewhat rowdy, and we quieter spirits therefore retired to a shady nook a little way up the creek, where, flat on our backs among the grass and ferns, we spent the early part of the afternoon yarning over other Christmas Days, spent in far different fashion in a far distant land. We too had Battle-axe brandy as a sort of afternoon tea, and this roused Dick up to such an extent that he burst forth into song. Unfortunately he chose for his theme, "The Old Folks at Home," and as we joined with his clear tenor in the chorus of the pathetic old song, there was a lump in more throats than mine as we thought of our old homes, and the very small chance the most of us had of seeing the dear old folks again. When the song was done, there was a dead pause, which no one seemed inclined to break, till Left-handed Bob astonished us by singing at the top of his voice, "Christians, Awake." We were mightily taken back and astonished, but somehow the grand Christmas hymn harmonized well with the surroundings,—the green grass, and ferns, and creepers, the trickling water, and the deep blue cloudless sky, and the murmur of sounds, softened by distance, which came up from the camp below made a splendid accompaniment.

As the afternoon wore away, and the shadows grew longer, some one suggested we should go up and visit old Father Maguire, whose labours, we opined, would probably be over for the day by this time. The holy father lived about a mile up the steep hillside in a small one-roomed hut, more than half hidden by great rocks and boulders, which in primeval ages some volcanic upheaval had scattered around. It was not very easy to find the father's hut at all; he might have been a priest of Reformation days, so hidden and secluded was his dwelling, and after partaking of the old man's hospitality, it was well-nigh impossible to find your way out of the maze again. As we approached, the volume of smoke that poured out of the chimney assured us our friend was holding high revel, and sure enough, when we opened the door, the atmosphere that rushed out was like that of an oven, for the place was barely fifteen feet square, and in the fireplace was a roaring fire, large enough to roast a bullock. In the middle of the room, on a small table on which were spread the remnants of a somewhat meagre feast, sat the owner of the cabin in his shirt sleeves, while beads of perspiration trickled down his jolly red face. His right hand grasped a pannikin, and his left beat time on the table to the strains of the "Shan Van Voght," which he was shouting at the top of his voice. Father Maguire was a kindly, jolly old soul, who loved not to mortify the flesh. The weekly Friday fasts were a sore trial to him; and it was rumoured, with what truth I know not, that he went down to the camp at Deadman's Creek, there to hold mass, and afterwards invariably called upon the Commissioner, who was not one of the faithful. That young gentleman was glad enough to entertain the jolly old priest, and always invited him to dinner, an invitation always cheerfully accepted, for the host was a man of taste, and his dinners, besides being abundant, had a refinement and a variety about them which most other dinners at that time lacked.

"By me sowl," Father Maguire would say, as he rose from the table, "by me sowl, but it's Friday, and it's meself has forgot that same." And as long as those dinners lasted the father continued to eat them, and invariably made the same remark afterwards. Peace be to his ashes—he has long since been gathered to his fathers. He was a jovial, merry old soul, fulfilling to the letter the Pauline behest, "to think no evil." and if he did eat some few more dinners than the rules of his Church allowed, good dinners did not often come in his way, and I trust he will not be hardly judged for them.

The moment he saw us he dropped the pannikin, and rose to greet us, a funny round tub of a man, with his braces dangling behind him.

"Och, sure, an' it's the bhoys! Come yez in, an' a merry Christmas to yez. Come yez in, an' I 'll brew yez some scaltheen in honor av the day."

Scaltheen was what Father Maguire was famous for, and exactly what we had come for. It was, in truth, rather a potent drink, consisting as it did of whisky, sugar, butter, and water, all boiled together in the little black kettle now singing away on the hob, and assisted materially in raising fresh difficulties round that already difficult path through the rocks.

As the old gentleman bustled round mixing his scaltheen, we became aware of another occupant of the cabin, a tall, thin, dark-haired, cadaverous-looking young priest, just fresh from All Hallows'. He sat there solemnly on an upturned brandy case in the corner, and glared disapprovingly out of his hollow black eyes at the revel going on round him. Father Maguire remembered his existence after a bit and introduced him.

"Sure an' it's Father Mahoney, bhoys, jist out from ould Ireland. Faix an' he's falin' a bit lonesome. Sure, now, Father dear, sing, sing—it'll do yez good. The 'Wearin' o' the Green,' Father, or 'Garry-owen.' Come now. His voice it's jist beautiful, bhoys; och, but ye should jist hear him," and the poor old father nodded confidentially at us, fell back in his chair, his eyes gradually closed, the pannikin dropped out of his hands, and the whiskey trickled down on to the earthen floor.

Father Mahoney evidently felt that the time had now come for him to speak or for ever after hold his peace, as the marriage service has it. He rose from his seat, and stalked across the room, a tall thin figure in his long black coat, and stood over his prostrate brother.

"Father Maguire," he said in the broadest of Cork brogues, without the ghost of a smile on his grave Irish face, "is it a song yez wantin'? Well, thin, it's just a jeremiad I 'd be singin' yez, an' not another song at all, at all."

Then, without deigning to take any notice of us, he flung open both door and window—the atmosphere stood greatly in need of a little freshening, I must admit—and went out on to the hillside, leaving us irreverent youngsters convulsed with laughter. The fun was over now as far as we were concerned, for Father Maguire, overcome by his own magic brew, was calmly sleeping, and no efforts of ours could elicit more than a grumpy, "Arrah, thin—be still now—will yez?"

So as the shadows were growing longer and longer, and Christmas Day was rapidly drawing to a close, we turned towards the camp again. Bob Wilson had spent rather a dreary afternoon all by himself, but we cheered him with a graphic account of our visit to the two priests, got him some tea, and then when the sun had set behind the hills, adjourned to the public house, the Eldorado Hotel as it was called, there to take part in one of those festive entertainments, known as a "Bull-dance "; that is to say, a dance at which women were conspicuous by their absence. In this case, though, we were in luck, for there were actually four women among about a hundred men, namely, the landlord's wife, a buxom matron of fifty, weighing about fourteen stone, but "game yet," as she herself said, "to shake a leg with the youngest;" his two daughters, fair, freckled, sandy-haired damsels, who were the objects of far greater attention than their very moderate charms appeared to sanction; and pretty Lizzie, the barmaid. We always called her "Pretty Lizzie," and if she had any other name I never heard it. She was a dainty little dark thing, with soft dark eyes and bright pink cheeks, and seemed somehow above her station. What adverse fate had drifted her into the service of old Long Potter I 'm sure I don't know, for she had bewitching ways, and a gentle voice that won all hearts. I don't think it was the absence of all feminine society that made us find "Pretty Lizzie" so specially charming. I even think, looking back now with all the accumulated wisdom of more than thirty years, that there was something wonderfully sweet about her. Anyhow, I, along with some hundred others, was very much in love with Lizzie, and, like them, had the pain of knowing—it was really a very keen pain in those days—that my love was unrequited.

The Eldorado was but a shanty, part calico tent, part corrugated iron. The room we danced in had only a hardwood floor, and for all furniture had a counter running across one end, on which were arrayed glasses, pannikins, and bottles, Behind this, Long Potter stood, dispensing refreshments to his guests, for which they paid in coin of the realm or gold dust. The music was provided by an old sailor with a fiddle and two concertinas, and if the guttering tallow candles and evil-smelling oil lamps did not provide light enough, outside was the glorious moon, now at the full, a round yellow disc poised in the dark, velvety sky. They were a rough crowd, those diggers, rowdy and foul-mouthed, and they squabbled not a little over their partners. First and foremost each man wanted to dance with Pretty Lizzie; Long Potter's two daughters came next, and failing them their buxom mother proved a bone of contention; the non-successful ones, and their name was legion, having to dance with each other.

And dance they did with a will. Never before or since have I seen such energetic dancing as we used to have at those bull-dances of diggings days. As the evening advanced and the liquor began to take effect, disputes became more frequent, disputes that were as a rule, promptly settled outside by a round of fisticuffs; but perhaps the best hated man there was the trooper, who came in about nine o'clock, and monopolized Pretty Lizzie. He was a big, fair man, this trooper—a gentleman evidently, down on his luck, as many a gentleman was in those days, and as evidently he was in love with Lizzie and she was in love with him. Oh, the adoring glances she cast at him as they went down the room together at a mad gallop. He got drunk as night advanced, and before I left I was dimly conscious of a dark corner where a sobbing woman was putting a pillow beneath the head of her insensible lover. Poor Pretty Lizzie, spite of it all, she married him; and ten years later I saw her again, the weary looking, draggle-tailed landlady of a wayside shanty, with half a dozen small children hanging on to her skirts and a drunken husband lolling in the bar. Poor Pretty Lizzie, she was worthy of a better fate.

I 'm afraid I must confess I don't remember much about the close of the evening. I wanted to dance with Lizzie, and when she would have none of me I consoled myself with the flowing bowl to such an extent that when by-and-by Dick, suggesting we should go home, took me by the arm and led me into the open air, I found the ground was rising up to meet me, and I remarked to my mate I thought that the moon must be getting old, she was so remarkably unsteady on her legs. I retired to my tent to wake up next morning with a splitting headache, as a pleasing reminiscence of the revel of the night before.

I am not a digger now. Long since I abandoned the pick and shovel for more lucrative employment—so long since that it is only occasionally I look back on my early days in the colony and my first Christmas on the diggings.

Milton Keynes UK
Ingram Content Group UK Ltd.
UKHW012250290324
440241UK00004B/279